A Sleigh Ride for Charlotte

SARAH LAMB

Contents

For each of you who loves but doesn't feel loved, I hope you'll find your happily ever after. Don't give up.

Chapter 1

1878 Spring Falls, Kansas

Charlotte hurried down the street, anxious to leave the excitement buzzing behind her. What was making others excited, giddy even, made her heart sink down to her worn boots that were crunching through the snow. Her throat constricted as she tried to force back the sob that begged to release.

Everywhere she went, young women stood in excited clusters, giggling and talking about the festival. Their words punctuated her steps.

"...deep purple, with puffy sleeves," one woman said as she paused for a wagon to cross the street.

"Mine will be deep red. Mother special ordered the fabric," another dreamily sighed. "It's heavenly."

She passed two men grinning and slapping each other on the back.

"...and then I'll ask her to marry me," one said. "Look at what I got her."

Charlotte dashed into the street and crossed to the other side before she could see what was in the box the man held, or hear another word about dresses.

Though she understood the joyous mood of the others, each and every word that her ears caught was like a wound to her already fragile heart.

She just wanted to go home. To hide and forget that in a few weeks, every single young woman in town—except for her—was going to be parading in their finest new dress, and getting chosen by one of the town's eligible men to join him for a sleigh ride...and a chance at romance.

The most romantic day of the year in Spring Falls, it was a time when many started courting and a few became engaged. Of course, that would never be Charlotte. Not when she couldn't even go to the festival.

Slowing her footsteps as the town faded behind her, Charlotte started the two-mile walk home. As she passed the trees heavy with new snowfall, she sighed. Was she overreacting? A friend had told her she was being silly. That you didn't have to attend the festival to find a beau. Charlotte knew that.

She also knew that she could attend even without a brand new dress. But why would she want to? Charlotte couldn't imagine being the only one there in a worn dress and shawl, looked upon with pity. She shook her head and pulled the offending garment closer.

Better to stay home. Best to not dare hope. Or dream. Dreams weren't for her. Not anymore. Not when they couldn't come true.

Charlotte had never attended the festival. It was one dream of many she'd given up on.

Truthfully, while it was the town's tradition, many of the courtships and flirting started well before the festival. The festival was just an excuse to take your relationship, or desire for one, to the next step. Most of the time the couple, or would-be couple, already had an inkling the other would approach them that day. Still, sometimes a young woman would bravely seek someone she'd had her eye on, and their romance blossomed.

Either way, it was something everyone she knew looked forward to. At one time, Charlotte had as well. But then circumstances changed, and her family was thrown into a difficult situation.

Still, a glimmer of hope had remained for her. The man she was interested in hadn't married or started courting yet. Even better, recently, he was said to have asked a friend if Charlotte had a beau. If he'd said that...could they possibly have a chance to get to know each other better? For her to be his pick for a sleigh ride?

Charlotte wanted that to be her. Longed for it. For nearly five years now, she sighed whenever she thought about August Middleton. They had attended school together, where she, along with every other girl, had admired him. August hadn't ever married nor seemed interested in any one woman. His sole focus was his family's businesses.

He was several years older than her, so finished school two years before Charlotte, and through a large inheritance from his father was well situated. He was so wealthy, her mother once commented that he left a trail of coins and heartbreak in his wake and never stopped to take notice of either.

Things might be different now, though. Perhaps he was ready to settle down with someone, and that's why he'd asked about her.

Her home rose ahead, and Charlotte felt herself relax. Home. The one place that she could be herself and not pretend. Pretend that all was well since Father had died. Since his partner had schemed and swindled and taken almost every cent they had.

Father, in his infinite goodness, had never once complained. They'd managed to keep their house, but there was very little else.

Though she couldn't really remember what his partner had looked like, for she'd been so young, Charlotte hoped that she'd never see that swindling man again. She'd give him a piece of her mind—and more! Father died of a broken heart, of that she had no doubt. Her dear mother, though she never said a cross or pitying word, had suddenly gone from being a well-off matron of the town to selling her beloved dresses, jewelry, and household items one at a time to put food on the table and clothes on their backs.

The house would be sold soon. Of that, Charlotte was certain. There was simply no way they could continue to keep it, not if they couldn't get more income.

"There you are," her mother said cheerfully as Charlotte approached. She was wrapped in her threadbare shawl on the porch. The shawl used to be her mother's Sunday best. Now, she simply went without one at church, unless it was so cold she was forced to wear something. "Did you have a nice walk?"

"Yes, but no luck getting a job," Charlotte said, stopping beside her. "There's nothing available."

"We will be fine, even without it," her mother said. "Do not worry yourself."

Charlotte wanted to argue, but they had done that before and it always ended the same, with Charlotte apologizing as soon as she saw the deep sadness in her mother's eyes. So, instead, she nodded and smiled. "I am quite sure you are right," she agreed. "Mrs. Luden at the bakery asked me to stop by next week if the girl she hired yesterday didn't work out."

"Wonderful," her mother answered. She smiled then. "I'll be inside soon. I just wanted to rest for a few moments and admire the snow. The trees are so pretty right now."

"Of course," Charlotte said. She patted her mother's hand. "I'm going to stir the soup and get warm."

As Charlotte walked inside, she couldn't help but feel a pang of regret and resentment. Her mother deserved better. She was so pale and weak. The doctor had said it was overwork and over worry. Charlotte couldn't agree more.

But this was their circumstance at the moment, and there was little they could do. And that was why Charlotte refused to let herself be laughed at if she went to the festival, and why she spent so little time in town. No, she would not be the poverty-stricken woman hoping to catch the eye of a man. She knew the one she wanted. He would also be the answer to a prayer.

What she needed to do was to learn if her friend was right, and he was interested in her too. August was always so busy. It might be that he had no idea of her family situation. If that was so, perhaps she could avoid the subject entirely.

Perhaps...perhaps there was a way to attract his attention. She could make something new to wear? Even a simple dress. Though she'd searched the house many times, and not once found anything she could use, maybe a miracle would happen and there would be fabric she had missed.

Slowly, Charlotte eyed each dress she had critically. Then, she studied the small box of her outgrown clothes. Bits here and there had been taken to make collars and cuffs and aprons until they were little more than scraps.

No. She had nothing. Just like always. Charlotte swallowed back both the lump burning in her throat and the tears that stung her eyes.

"Charlotte?"

Her mother's soft voice had her wiping her eyes quickly. "Yes, Mama?" she asked.

"Whatever is wrong, my dear?" her mother asked softly, sitting next to her on her bed. "Is it the job?"

"It's nothing at all," Charlotte lied.

But her mother knew, as she always did. Sadness creased her face. "Have they announced the date for the festival?" she asked.

"Yes," Charlotte hiccupped. "Everyone was clustered around talking about it. Looking forward to it."

"Will you go?" her mother asked.

"Of course not," Charlotte answered. She hoped her voice wasn't bitter sounding, but she couldn't be sure.

They sat quietly for a long time. This was the third year in a row they'd had this conversation. Her mother let out a long sigh. "I understand. I dislike you keeping to yourself and wrapped in sadness because you can't have the kind of experience that you hope for, but I understand. Truth be told, I wouldn't want to go either, were I in your shoes."

It wasn't just the festival and the desire for a dress. It was also the cloud of self-pity that kept trying to hover over her head, no matter how many times she pushed it aside. Charlotte didn't want to feel that way. She didn't. But despair was starting to fill her, and worry. Even if they sold the house and moved to a smaller one, how much longer could they manage? The situation was getting difficult.

"It will be fine," Charlotte said. The lies were coming too easily. Did that mean she'd given up hope of things ever getting better?

"What of August? I thought you mentioned he was interested in you," her mother said.

"It's only what I heard from Betty," Charlotte admitted. "I've not seen him yet to know. But, wouldn't that be wonderful? We would be well off again!"

"My dear, seeking a match only for a better financial situation isn't a good idea. You need to find someone you can love and who loves you. There's always been something about August that was...off-putting to me. Makes me worried. You understand, I only want what's best for you."

Charlotte knew her mother was right. But sometimes, she thought she'd settle for anyone if it put her and her mother in a better financial situation. In fact, if she couldn't figure out a way to help them soon, she might even consider becoming a mail-order bride—with the stipulation her mother came with her.

"Never you mind, dear. We'll plan a cozy evening in. All will be well, and perhaps next year you'll attend." Her mother squeezed her hand and left the room.

She, too, was lying, Charlotte knew. They were both well aware next year would be the same as this one, perhaps even worse.

Especially if August Middleton wasn't interested in her. There was no one else who would ever make her happy. This, Charlotte knew.

Chapter 2

Dr. Justin Davis stood, his hands on his hips, and nodded in satisfaction. It had taken nearly a full day, but the office—his office—was looking much more how he wanted it. Dr. Jeffers had sold him the practice when he decided to retire, and it was obvious that the man hadn't changed a single thing in the entire time he'd been practicing there.

Luckily, the large wooden desk and sturdy chairs in the waiting room were fine, as was the examination table. The rest, though...

A few faded paintings had gone into a box, as well as a large stuffed squirrel that had been hung on the wall. Dr. Jeffers, luckily, wanted the deer antlers that had hung over the doorway. Justin replaced them with a small bell on some twine that would jangle softly when someone entered.

Dr. Jeffers hadn't taken all of his personal equipment, but Justin had brought with him his own medical instruments, and had carefully packed away what he wouldn't use. While the items he stored were older and worn, they still had value in them to a potential assistant or someone wishing to learn more about medicine.

He stretched, gave one more satisfied nod, and then went over to a large crate. It was so heavy it had taken two men to load it into a wagon and two to bring it in. After prying off the lid, Justin tackled the pile of medical books inside. Carefully, he set each on the large bookcase near his desk, then nodded in approval once he was done. Yes, it was all coming together nicely.

Spring Falls seemed to be just what he wanted. It was growing, was large enough to support a goodly number of businesses, and not so far from Cottonwood Falls that he couldn't have urgent supplies sent quickly, should the need arise. There was also another doctor there, Edward Mason, who he could consult with if needed. He'd gone and met him and his wife, Caroline, before purchasing this practice, and had bought a few supplies from the large store there.

There was only one thing missing now, and that was an assistant. Old Dr. Jeffers had his wife as nurse, and she had no intention of staying. Not that he'd have wanted her, anyway. No, what Justin wanted was someone who he could train to do things the way he wanted them. When one took on a nurse who had years of experience, they often had their own methods and ways of doing things. The last thing he wanted, as a practice owner and someone new to town, was to butt heads and upset someone because he had his preferences and, to be quite honest, newer methods of providing care than some of the older doctors might be familiar with.

Nearing thirty, and having spent three years working for another doctor, he was ready to have his own practice, take all he'd learned, and set it up just how he wanted.

The door opened, and the small bell tinkled. Justin looked over. "Dr. Jeffers," he greeted eagerly.

"Thought I'd see how you were coming along, if you were settling in well," the doctor said.

"There is one thing I could use your advice on, actually," Justin said. "I'd put an ad in the paper, but there have been no inquiries yet. Before I take out another, or expand to the newspaper in Cottonwood Falls, perhaps you know. Is there someone I could hire as a competent nurse? If you needed one, it is likely I will as well."

Dr. Jeffers grew a thoughtful look, then scratched his head. "I don't think so," he said slowly. "What you might even look for is someone to help with your notes and files, and then perhaps one day train them to take on small tasks, like helping bandage wounds or collect medications for you to approve before they are sent home with a patient."

"I was worried that might be the case," Justin sighed. "Perhaps I'll ask around, but if I've not found someone by the end of the week, I'll resubmit my ad, and perhaps to a few towns."

"I'm sorry," Dr. Jeffers said. "Hopefully, you manage until you find someone. There was a quiet day here and there, but for the most part, Mrs. Jeffers and I stayed quite busy. Do you want me to ask if she'd be willing to come an afternoon a week?"

"No, no," Justin said. "You need to enjoy your retirement. Travel around and visit your children."

He couldn't imagine how much help one afternoon a week would be. It might even make things worse. The doctor was right. What he needed, if he couldn't find a nurse, was at least someone to help with notes and files.

Files. The word brought to mind another question.

"Dr. Jeffers, I noticed that this file here has a star in the upper corner," Justin said, going over to his desk and holding it up. He'd spent almost an entire day going over each file and note to familiarize himself with the patients the other doctor had seen.

The old doctor walked over and took the file, squinting at it. "That's right. She's a special case."

"Special in what way?" Justin queried. "When I went through it, she seemed to be quite ordinary, as far as care."

"Yes," the doctor said slowly. "That's Mrs. Harrison."

The combination of the weight behind his words and the tone of his voice made Justin search the doctor's face. "I sense a story," he remarked.

"A sad one," Dr. Jeffers said. "A terrible thing happened to the Harrisons. It's why I don't charge Mrs. Harrison for her care. Of course, you are not obligated to continue that tradition. Nor would she expect you to."

Justin sat behind his desk and motioned for Dr. Jeffers to sit as well. "What happened?" he asked.

The doctor's face filled with sorrow. "Jim Harrison was my best friend. We went to school together growing up and went our own ways to university. I became a doctor, of course, but Jim always had a love for the written word. He decided to follow in his father's footsteps in publishing.

"Well, some twenty years later, we met back up, having moved here near the same time. It was wonderful to reconnect with him. Jim had married by then," he pointed to the folder, "and about a year later, Pricilla had a daughter."

"I'm not sensing anything tragic about that, unless something happened to their child?" Justin asked.

"No, no. Charlotte has grown up into a lovely young woman. One of the prettiest in town, but also one of the most kind and practical. She's going to make some man a fine wife one day."

"Then what happened?" Justin asked.

"Wasn't long after they moved here that Jim took on a partner for his publishing business. Jim would travel back and forth regularly, but that became less and less as his partner did more. I don't know all the details of how it all happened, but one day, Jim got tricked into signing something."

"Oh no." Justin frowned.

"That's right," Dr. Jeffers agreed. "That partner of his swindled him out of just about everything. The business got signed over to him. All the profit went to him. Every bit except for the royalties that remained from a few books his father had published years before. That couldn't be touched, as it was in his will. Doubt it brings in much."

"That poor family," Justin said. "Nothing could be done?"

"Don't think so," Dr. Jeffers said heavily. "Jim died of a broken heart and guilt when Charlotte was about ten. Pricilla had a real hard time of it. Poor woman has struggled to keep food on the table, but she refuses to accept help. I suspect their savings is all gone, and I don't know how she survives, honestly."

"That's a terrible story," Justin said. "My heart breaks for them." He sighed and rubbed the bridge of his nose. "However, if I give charity to one, others will expect it."

"That is why you must decide for yourself if you will continue to treat her at no charge," Dr. Jeffers said. "Though I think most folks would understand if word got out, others might not, and you must be able to provide for yourself."

Dr. Jeffers stood then, and smacked the desk. "Well, I've got to be going. If you should need anything, you know where to find me."

"Yes, and thank you," Justin said. A pit of disappointment filled him. He should have asked the doctor to stay for tea. Perhaps tell him more. The office seemed incredibly empty, and it was difficult moving to a town and not knowing anyone in it.

His eyes followed the doctor as he walked down the street. A young woman with strawberry-blonde hair passed, and Justin let his eyes linger on her. For some reason he couldn't explain, he felt drawn to her. As if she felt someone staring at her, she paused and glanced around before resuming her trek.

Justin watched her graceful steps on the snowy sidewalk. She was beautiful and held herself with confidence. He wondered who she was. The woman entered a store, and he turned back to the file and sighed.

What to do about this patient? He didn't want to be thought of as cold. Perhaps he could still provide the medical care this woman and her daughter needed. After all, it was likely very little.

"But, perhaps I should also see that for myself before deciding," he said to the papers before him. "I'll introduce myself, explain I am taking over the practice. Getting to know people."

The idea felt right. Justin grabbed his coat and hat, then decided to take his traveling doctor's bag, just in case.

As he set out, the young woman with the strawberry-blonde hair was coming out of the general store. Her face was filled with disappointment. He didn't know why, he certainly didn't know her, but Justin felt a pang of sympathy in his chest. Something must have happened for her to look so dejected.

To his surprise, the young woman squared her shoulders, visibly took a deep breath, put on a smile, and then went into the bakery. Justin started to linger, but realized he had no business doing so. His patient was waiting for him. Whatever it was the young woman sought, he hoped she found it. She didn't deserve to wear such sadness on her face.

Chapter 3

Charlotte pulled her shawl closer around her. The wind had picked up, and snow flurries were starting to fly through the air. Her trip to town felt wasted. Once again, there were no positions available. At the general store, they decided they were managing just fine, as the store's sales were dropping off due to the cold weather.

The bakery quite liked the work of the other young woman they'd hired, and planned to continue with her. Charlotte had checked two more places, the dressmaker and the diner, but no one needed help.

Right now, she felt discouraged. And cold. She quite looked forward to getting inside the house, where the stove in the kitchen would be warming the kettle. A bit of tea would be welcome.

A sigh escaped. They'd been drinking tea of their own making for so long, she missed the stronger brew her mother would buy at the general store when she was a girl. But they had no money for it, and the herbs and wildflowers provided a pleasant flavor, even if weak at times. It was better than plain water, which they would drink once their supply of what they picked ran out. Spring, and new plant growth, felt so far away.

This last summer, they'd grown peppermint and carefully dried each leaf. A cup of that was what she craved now. Warm and minty. Especially the warm part. Though it wouldn't ease her worry over not finding work, perhaps she could just curl up with a bit of sewing, watch the snow, and try to forget her worries.

Her legs sped up just a little more until she was almost breathless as the house came into view. Her shivering was getting almost uncontrollable as the snowflakes melted on her head, dampening her hair.

Charlotte pushed the front door open and hurried into the kitchen. "Goodness, Mama! It's so cold outside," she said as she unwound her shawl.

And then she froze. Her mother wasn't alone. A man, a handsome one at that, looked up at her, and then rose from his chair.

"Hello," Charlotte greeted, giving her mother a puzzled look. She'd never seen him before. Luckily, her mother introduced him before her mind wandered too much.

"Charlotte, dear, this is Dr. Justin Davis. He's taking over for Dr. Jeffers, and came out to introduce himself." Her mother smiled at the doctor. "He was also kind enough to bring his bag in case I wasn't feeling well."

"That's incredibly thoughtful of you," Charlotte said, moving closer to the stove. She hoped her mother was feeling well. She wouldn't put it past her to dismiss any health problems she might have. "It's a pleasure to meet you, Doctor."

She tried not to stare as she turned to face him, but the doctor was quite unlike anyone else she'd ever seen. His clothes were much nicer than those most of the men around here wore, except for August. His voice also had a slight accent she couldn't place. He had light-brown hair that curled slightly on the top.

Warm brown eyes met hers, and he smiled. "It's good to meet you. I've been enjoying your mother's information about the town. I'm new to Kansas, and so far everyone has been kind and welcoming."

"Oh! Where are you from?" Charlotte asked as she poured herself a cup of tea, pleased to note it was the mint. "I thought you had a slight accent." She settled at the table.

"Virginia," he answered. "Born, raised, and educated."

"Goodness, that must have been quite a trip here," Charlotte said in surprise.

"It was, but I enjoyed it. I met quite a few interesting people on the way, and I had the anticipation of starting my practice." Dr. Davis turned his lips up again. His eyes lit when he smiled, she noticed. His expression was genuine, not one that looked forced.

"How did you learn of Dr. Jeffers selling his practice?" Charlotte's mother asked.

"His father knew my father, and during one of the letters they exchanged, he mentioned that he was considering retirement, and asked Father to listen for anyone who might be interested. So," he laughed, "here I am, though much to my mother's dismay."

"I am sure." Charlotte's mother nodded. "Yet, our town is most grateful for her sacrifice. Be sure you tell her I said so. We need a doctor, and one familiar with the newest medicines and treatments will be most welcome. Out here, anything could happen, from an animal bite to an accident to a gunshot wound. You'll need every bit of your education."

"I'm looking forward to whatever challenges come my way," the doctor said. "Though..." He hesitated then, and an uncertain look grew over his face.

"What is it?" Charlotte's mother asked, concerned.

Charlotte also felt a twinge of worry. Whatever was so terrible that a doctor was hesitant to speak of it?

Dr. Davis shrugged and admitted, "Well, perhaps you might be able to help me. You know the townsfolk better than I do. I'm looking for someone to act as my nurse. If she has no medical capability, I'd be more than content to have someone simply copy my notes and assist with the office side of my practice. I could teach her things as they came up. So far, I've had no answers to my advertisements. Would you happen to know of anyone trustworthy? It is a paying position."

Charlotte's eyes widened, and she sucked in a breath. Her mother glanced at her and raised her eyebrow. Charlotte gave the smallest of nods. This could be it. A job! A distinguished one, as well.

"My daughter is quite trustworthy," her mother said, "and has also been seeking employment. Perhaps…"

The doctor turned and met her eyes. He studied her for a moment. "Is that so? I admit, it isn't the most exciting of jobs, and I'm afraid that the social aspect will be limited, unlike working in a shop."

"I don't care about that," Charlotte said quickly. "I'd be grateful for an opportunity to try. I took care of my father in his poor health, and though that isn't quite the same as being a nurse, I think I would be competent enough to learn to help you, if you'll let me attempt it."

He smiled at her, that warm look filled his face, and he glanced between her and her mother. "Then I would be most delighted to see if we are a good fit together, as long as you both agree."

"Of course! You also must stay for an early dinner," Charlotte's mother pronounced, jumping up. "Then, you can tell Charlotte more of the details of the job and what you need, so when she starts, she is as prepared as possible."

"Oh, I couldn't intrude," Dr. Davis said, shaking his head.

"Nonsense." Charlotte rose from the table. "We are having potato and kale soup. There's plenty. It's just the sort of thing for a cold day like this."

"It is cold," the doctor agreed. Then he added, "I'd be grateful for the companionship. I've not made the acquaintance of many in town, and my evenings have been spent either reading medical journals or writing letters home."

"Then it's settled," her mother announced. "Charlotte, you slice the bread and I will ladle the soup. It's ready now."

In no time at all, they were sitting around the small kitchen table. Warmth filled Charlotte, from the stove heating the space, the soup, and the idea of a job. She wondered what he would pay. Not that she'd ask; that would be impolite. But perhaps...Charlotte bit her lip. Perhaps there might be enough for some fabric for a new dress. A festival dress.

"My word, Mrs. Harrison. This is the best soup I've ever eaten," the doctor exclaimed.

Charlotte smiled as her mother blushed. The doctor was kind, in more ways than one. She appreciated that. He was truthful, though. One would never guess the rich soup was so inexpensive to make.

"I'm glad you enjoy it. It was my late husband's favorite." Her mother's voice caught, but only for a moment.

"I'm honored, then, that I got to enjoy it in the fine company of his family," Dr. Davis said, without any hint of falsehood.

The rest of the meal passed quicker than she'd have liked as they discussed the aspects of her new job, and Charlotte's mother answered the doctor's many questions about their town.

Charlotte found she was enjoying the doctor's company. It was clear her mother was as well. It was nice to have someone new to talk to. He was good at conversation, and had a relaxed, easy way about him that she liked.

When the sun lowered and they said goodbye, he bundled against the cold and set back toward town. Charlotte turned to her mother as she watched him wave goodbye from the road and smiled. "What an afternoon this has turned out to be. I was quite disappointed that there were no jobs to be found in town, and now this! I think I shall enjoy working for the new doctor."

"He seems a good man," her mother agreed. "It will be a help for us and for him. You'll do a fine job."

"Mama," Charlotte said, almost afraid to ask. "If he pays me enough, do you think I might...No. No, I can't ask."

"You don't need to," her mother said firmly. "Yes. I expect you to take some of your earnings to buy some fabric for a dress, dear. After all, it will keep me busy piecing it together and then sewing while you are working. I must have something to do."

Charlotte hugged her mother in delight. She could scarcely believe it. For the first time in years, it felt like something was finally going right.

With a new job, and a chance for a new dress, why she'd surely be able to catch August Middleton's eye. And then, once she did, things would simply continue to get better. Perhaps in just a few months, she'd no longer be Charlotte Harrison, but Mrs. Charlotte Middleton.

Chapter 4

Shaking off his coat, Justin hung it on a peg and then rubbed his hands together. As cold as he was in his warm coat that was only two years old, he couldn't imagine how chilled Miss Harrison had been when she came home with only that thin shawl.

Hiring her, on a trial basis of course, had been the right thing to do. This would be a mutual benefit. She and her mother needed the financial help. He needed someone in his office. The arrangement had nothing to do with the way his heart had sped up when joy had lit her eyes, or how beautiful her smile was.

No. Nothing at all.

He rubbed his frozen hands together to warm them. It was far colder here than back home. There weren't many trees out on the prairies, so when the wind whipped, it rushed straight through everything in its path. The chill in the air was hard to shake, and Justin wouldn't lie—he was eager for spring to come.

A shout from outside caught his attention, and he glanced out the window to see two young men running away from a sign tacked on the general store across the street. He squinted at it.

"Winter festival. Huh." He'd have to ask Miss Harrison about that. There weren't too many details on the sign, at least, not that he could read from this distance. Him being new in town, and not really knowing too many people, perhaps he'd go.

Perhaps Miss Harrison would go with him. Justin wouldn't lie, he was more than delighted that the lovely young woman he'd seen walking through town was his new assistant, and he'd not only been able to make her acquaintance, but also now would spend more time with her. He intended to do all he could to keep the smiles on her face, not the sad expression he'd seen each time he'd spotted her previously.

Now that he knew the story of her father, that explained a lot. That family had suffered a great deal. They seemed so nice. He'd felt guilty accepting Mrs. Harrison's offer of dinner, worrying it might take food that they needed from them, but he enjoyed their company so much, and it was obvious they enjoyed his. Since he planned to hire Miss

Harrison—and now pay her perhaps a bit more than he'd intended—he let his discomfort dissipate.

Besides, it had been quite an incredible soup. So simple, yet so filling and nourishing.

Snow began to fall in earnest now, illuminated by someone here or there passing with a lantern. The last of the sun's rays were gone, and the stores were closed. He was grateful he didn't have to seek his dinner at the diner or figure out how to make something for himself.

It had been a long two weeks getting the office situated, seeing patients on the outskirts of town, and seeking nonstop for a nurse. Thankfully, he now had one, or at least someone who could lighten the patient load, and he wouldn't have to work at such a frantic pace. Having someone to help here set his mind at ease.

Justin went through the locked door in the back storage room and up a flight of steps to where his rooms were. He had two. A bedroom and a larger room that served as a kitchen, dining room, and sitting room. It was rather convenient. The Jeffers had a house elsewhere, and this was just used on occasion when they had to stay overnight in town.

The furniture was nearly new, and the bed quite comfortable. He appreciated it very much right now as he stretched out and yawned. It felt good to rest. His body was tired.

So, why wasn't his mind? Why did it race around and around, thinking about Charlotte Harrison? Each time he closed his eyes, her beautiful face swam in front of him. Her voice was pleasing to his ears, and if he concentrated hard enough, he could almost hear her.

While she hadn't spoken much during the meal, when she had, it was obvious that she was intelligent and thoughtful in her answers. She'd make a fine nurse. He would enjoy her company as well.

Though he would be busy with patients, it would be nice to have someone to talk with between appointments or on quiet days. Justin wouldn't admit it to anyone else, but sometimes it was a little lonely being a doctor. While everyone was polite, there was a...distance that they kept.

It was necessary, but made it hard to develop friendships. Before he'd left, his peers had warned him that unless he lived in a place with other doctors, he might find the company he kept was mostly his own or that of his wife. Since he didn't have a wife, it had been a little lonely the last few weeks.

Perhaps having Miss Harrison here would change that.

He stilled suddenly. Why was it she popped into his head at almost every moment? He'd only just met her! What on earth was his mind doing? His thoughts were bordering on highly inappropriate. She was an employee. Perhaps one day a friend. It would—could—go no further.

The night passed slowly. At last, his mind stilled and he fell asleep to the sound of the wind's whistle. His office was sturdy, so he let the sound soothe him, and eventually, perhaps even too soon, morning came.

From his bed, Justin could see the first hint of dawn. He admired it for a moment, then reluctantly rose. Suddenly, he remembered. Today, Miss Harrison would arrive.

Dressing quickly, he put on the kettle and ate some bread and cheese. As he went down the stairs and checked the time, he saw the bakery opening. Justin grabbed his coat and ran across the street and down several buildings.

As he let himself into the warm storefront, he breathed deeply. There was the perfect blend of yeasty bread, freshly baked sweet rolls, savory pies, and cakes.

"Good morning, Doctor," the baker said as he carried a large tray of apple fritters. "What can I get for you this morning?"

"Ahhh..." Justin stood.

What should he get? What would Miss Harrison enjoy?

"May I have a moment to think?" he asked. "It all looks quite good."

"It is," a voice said, and a man walked closer.

Justin recognized the sheriff and nodded hello.

"I'll take two apple fritters," Sheriff Asher Steele said as he set two mugs on the counter. "Oh, and Jeff wants a sausage roll. I'll take one as well."

"You got it," the baker said, and set to filling the order and the coffees in the mugs.

"Settling in?" the sheriff asked Justin.

"I am, and I've even found a local young woman to help in my office," Justin replied.

"Good," Sheriff Steele remarked. "If you ever need me, or think I can help, I'm across the street."

"Thank you, Sheriff," Justin said.

Sheriff Steele left, and the baker asked, "Decided what you'd like?"

"Yes," he answered. "Let me have a half dozen of your muffins. You choose which."

The baker filled a brown bag, and after he paid, Justin returned to his office. He set the bag on his desk and checked the time again. He'd be opening soon. That meant Miss Harrison would arrive.

As if he'd thought her into existence, his door opened, and the bell tinkled. "Good morning," Miss Harrison said with a slightly nervous smile. "I hope I'm not late."

"Not at all," Justin said. "I am glad you are here. Let me show you around before the first patient arrives."

During the next few minutes, he took her around the small office. First, he showed her the desk she was to use, then the examination room. She peeked into the storeroom, and then followed him upstairs where he kept the small stove, kettle, and mugs she was allowed to use.

"It's all so very tidy," she said as they came back down the stairs.

"I'll need your help to keep it that way," Justin admitted. "It's been difficult on my own."

"I am happy to be here, Doctor, and I thank you," she said. "I will do all that I can to assist you with whatever you need."

"Ah, Justin is fine, when we are not around patients," he said quickly. "There's no need to be so formal. We are in the West, after all. Aren't things more relaxed here? And we are so similar in age, I'd rather us speak as though we are friends."

She looked at him, surprised, but then nodded. "You must call me Charlotte, then."

"Charlotte," he repeated. His heart sped up again as he spoke her name. His mouth grew dry, and he glanced about for some water.

"I can start to copy your notes now," she offered.

"Yes, that would be good," he said.

As Charlotte settled into her desk, the first patient of the day arrived. Justin led the patient to the examination room, trying to focus on what the man was telling him about his aching back.

Perhaps hiring an assistant wasn't a good idea. He hadn't realized just how distracting having Charlotte here would be.

Chapter 5

Charlotte smiled to herself as she looked out the window of the doctor's office. The morning had gone well, and she hoped that as her days continued here, that they would be just as enjoyable and that the doctor would decide to keep her on.

That morning, she'd left home a few moments early, eager to stare into the general store windows before she started work. To her delight, the fabric was being restocked. As soon as she received her first pay, she planned to buy herself a dress length of whatever caught her eye. The idea of being able to select something new had kept her up half the night with excitement. It had been so long since she'd had a new dress. Now that it was within her grasp, it was hard not to think about it.

Her mother didn't know it, but Charlotte planned to buy fabric to make her a dress as well. Later would be the purchase of a new shawl for each of them. This new job would help in so many ways. It gave them opportunity. She wouldn't squander it, and planned to work as hard as she could for the doctor.

Dr. Davis, or Justin as he was letting her call him, was very kind, and she felt at ease around him. Once she'd arrived, he'd taken her on a tour of the office, shown just what he needed her help with first, and then offered her muffins he'd bought at the bakery. He was even trusting her enough to go upstairs to his living quarters to make tea if she desired.

She planned to make sure there was always hot water so that he could have a drink at a moment's notice. He seemed to have trouble adjusting to the drier air, as she observed him stopping often for a sip of water.

Without a doubt, she was having a much easier time with his job than she would have had in the bakery. There, she was sure she'd have been run near ragged. The baker was just fine, but his wife was a taskmaster.

The examination room door opened, and the doctor walked out with his young patient, a child of four who looked momentarily distracted by a penny candy the doctor had especially for children.

"Thank you, Doctor," a tired-looking mother said as she put her arm around the coughing child.

"Of course. I'll come around in two days to check on him. If he worsens, send for me right away. Until then, keep that chest warm, and have him drink plenty of peppermint tea." The doctor added, "Remember to look after yourself as well."

The mother and her child left, and Justin sighed as he watched them go. "That poor woman. Her husband is away driving cattle. It's their only child, and she's quite worried about his cough."

"It didn't sound good," Charlotte agreed.

"No, there is a little wheezing. I think perhaps the cold air has caused it. There is a chronic condition that happens at times called asthma. It can be triggered by not just the cold, but things like dust or smoke." Justin stared out the window thoughtfully. "Hopefully, there is no worsening."

Charlotte studied him a moment. Though she hardly knew the doctor, just from observing his interactions with patients he'd seen this morning, she could see how much he cared about them. He was diligent, took the time the patient needed to feel looked after, and was friendly to each. Some people, she suspected, simply wanted someone to talk to. He seemed not only able to help the healing of their bodies, but also their hearts.

Her mother was right, he seemed a good man. Though she'd felt that from the moment she'd first met him, working here only confirmed the fact.

A movement outside the window drew her attention, and Charlotte's heart sped up while her stomach started to do flips. It was August!

She sat up straight and focused her attention on him. He was walking into the general store. August was so tall, he always strode with a sort of determination when he walked. A confidence. And why not? His family was wealthy, and that confidence was likely because he knew there was nothing he lacked. If there was, he could get it, easily.

Which was why it was a bit of a mystery that he'd never married. He could have his pick of anyone he wanted. It had always been that way, yet, whenever he'd stepped out with a girl while they were in school, it never lasted long.

Charlotte was determined to change that. She just needed a chance.

The general store door closed behind him, and she sighed as he vanished from view.

"Everything okay?" Justin asked, looking over at her.

She startled, having momentarily forgotten she wasn't alone. "Yes, just...tired," Charlotte said. She smiled at him. "I was so excited last night to be here today, I didn't sleep well."

He grinned at her. It was a friendly look, and she appreciated it. She was glad the doctor wasn't bossy or stuffy. Instead, he felt like a friend. That would make her days much easier.

"Same," he admitted. "I'm still getting used to the town's sounds at night and the new bed."

"I am sure you will settle in soon," Charlotte answered, letting her eyes wander to the store again.

August hadn't come out yet.

"What do you find so fascinating out there?" the doctor asked, moving closer to the window.

"Oh." Charlotte flushed, a little embarrassed at being caught. "I was...I was just looking at the festival sign."

The office door opened just then, and a man rushed in, groaning. "Doc! Doc! I think I broke my arm."

Justin wasted no time. "Come with me," he said, hurrying into his examination room.

As he led the man away, Charlotte saw August exit the general store with a friend, mount his horse, and leave. She watched until he was out of sight, then sighed softly and bent her head back over the doctor's notes she was copying. She hoped that there would be an opportunity to talk with him soon.

If her friend had been right and he'd asked about her, did that mean he was hoping to bump into her? She hoped so. How could she make an opportunity for that? Perhaps at church?

August was—

"Charlotte. I need your assistance," Justin said, sticking his head out of the examination room. "We need to put Mr. Smith's shoulder back into place."

Swallowing hard, Charlotte nodded, hoping the expression on her face was calm. She'd never done such a thing and hoped she didn't make a mistake that would make the poor, suffering man feel worse. "I'm coming now," she said.

When she entered the room, a wave of concern rocked in her stomach. Mr. Smith looked as though he was in a good deal of pain. Beads of sweat were on his forehead, even though the room wasn't warm. "How can I help?" she asked.

"Mr. Smith has dislocated his shoulder. I will do the work. I want you to help hold him still," the doctor replied calmly.

Charlotte nodded and bit her lip. She held Mr. Smith the way she was told, and a few moments later, there was a jolting sound, a scream from Mr. Smith, and then silence.

She wasn't sure which had scared her the most. Charlotte tried to keep her face calm, but she wasn't sure she could. Mr. Smith was lying there, his eyes closed. Had they...was he...

"Ah, much better, Doc," the man said suddenly, springing up from the table. "I thank ye kindly."

"Of course," Justin answered, and together they walked out into the main room.

Charlotte stayed behind, one hand pressed to her stomach and a light feeling in her head. She allowed herself to close her eyes a moment and willed her swirling stomach to calm. She could hear the door's bell tinkle as Mr. Smith left, and a moment later a hand was on her arm.

"Charlotte, are you well? Perhaps you should sit."

She nodded and opened her eyes. "I apologize," she told the doctor. Her voice sounded unsteady to her ears. "That was new. And different. And unexpected."

Justin was looking at her with concern. "If the job is too much—"

"No!" she interrupted. "No, I apologize. This won't happen again. Please," she said, realizing her voice had risen in panic, "I want this job."

"It is yours, for as long as you'd like it," he assured her. "I apologize. It was not something I could do alone easily."

"I think next time I will do better," Charlotte said. She pulled her hand from her stomach. "I believe what startled me was when he laid there unmoving after you'd pulled his shoulder back into place."

Justin laughed. "Yes! That quite shook me up for a moment as well. I didn't know what to think. Between the two of us, mentally, I was frantically flipping pages of my medical journals to recall such a thing."

A feeling of relief washed over her, and she giggled. "That makes me feel better. I promise to keep that secret."

The door to his office opened again, and a voice called, "Doc?"

"I'm right here. Oh! Sheriff Steele, what can I do for you?" the doctor asked.

"We've got a prisoner in the jail. Was holding him during the stage stop. He's complaining about his head. Could you come take a look?" Sheriff Steele caught sight of Charlotte and nodded at her.

"Of course," Justin said, and grabbed his travel bag he kept near the door. "Charlotte, I'll be back soon. Please let any patients know that."

He left before she could answer. Charlotte returned to her desk. Alone, her eyes roamed out the window again and to the sign for the festival. A smile spread over her face.

This was the year she'd be in the festival. This was also the year that she'd find love. She just knew it. She had the doctor to thank for this chance at both.

Chapter 6

"Here you are, Doctor," the young woman at the bakery said, her eyes fluttering at him. Did she perhaps have something in her eye? He wasn't sure, but thought she might just ask him to look, the way she was blinking. As a doctor, he was used to not being able to walk down the street or browse a store without someone mentioning some ailment.

When she didn't mention her eye, he accepted the bag, having already paid. "Thank you," he said politely and turned to the door.

"Doctor," the woman started.

He looked back at her, ready for her question. He didn't see any redness in her eye, but perhaps when she—

"Are you going to the festival with anyone?" she asked.

Now it was his turn to blink rapidly. His reaction, however, was one of surprise at the sudden topic change. "The festival? I'm afraid I'm not sure yet."

"Oh." The disappointment was clear on her face.

Someone else entered the bakery, and Justin took the opportunity to leave. When Charlotte arrived, he needed to ask her more about this festival. Though he'd passed posters for it several times, the details were sparse.

Perhaps whatever it was would be something Charlotte would like to attend with him. The idea wasn't unappealing. In fact, he could easily see that he'd enjoy it. Though she'd only been working for him about two weeks, he enjoyed each moment with her.

Charlotte had quickly picked up on what he needed her to do around the office. She was good with the patients, and they enjoyed chatting with her. Her handwriting was neat and easy to read, and she did an impeccable job at keeping the office clean. The times he'd needed her assistance, she'd done so calmly and watched closely to learn all she could. Justin could count on Charlotte to anticipate and prepare what medical items he'd request or ask her to send home with a patient.

He appreciated her very much. Which was in part why he'd taken to getting her a muffin or other baked good each morning. He'd like to do something more, something to help her and her mother, but he wasn't sure if propriety would allow it.

It was difficult, as he must be mindful of appearances. Charlotte, being both unmarried and lovely, had a reputation he knew could be ruined at any sign of behavior that one might take as a sign he was pressuring her for favors or giving her unwanted attention. That could also be an unwelcome thing for his business.

Justin jogged the last few steps to his office and opened the door. He set the bag from the bakery on her desk, ensuring it would be there when she arrived, and then reached into his pocket to place an envelope down containing her pay.

The door opened, and she hurried inside, smiling. "Good morning," she said cheerfully.

"Good morning," he replied, trying very hard not to stare at her. Her cheeks were pink this morning, and she looked excited about something. It would be rude of him to ask what, but he did wonder.

"What's this?" Charlotte asked, touching the envelope.

"That is your pay," Justin answered. "The other bag is a warm pumpkin muffin."

"Oh!" she said, her face lighting up. "Thank you for both!" She met his eyes. "I'm really enjoying my job. Thank you again for offering it to me."

"You've been an incredible help," Justin told her honestly. "I am glad you are here. You have made my job much easier, and for that I am grateful."

She smiled at him again, that smile he knew he'd do anything to see again and again, and tucked the envelope into her handbag. "When we have our lunch, or else at the end of the day, I'm going to go across to the general store. I plan to take part of this and get Mama and I each fabric for a new dress."

Charlotte laughed and shook her head. "That sounds silly perhaps, but neither of us have had one since Papa passed away. There's enough in here to help with necessities, and celebrate my new job."

His eyes widened, and Justin was glad Charlotte wasn't looking at him. For over ten years, she'd not had a new dress? He didn't know too much about those things, being male, but he was sure it was a difficult, even upsetting or embarrassing thing for a young woman to wear a dress given to her that someone else had worn, or to continually make over old fabric.

Yet, she didn't have a depressed state about her. Charlotte always seemed happy, content. He admired that, even if he still wanted to do more for her.

He glanced out the window to see if his first patient was scurrying along, and his gaze fell on the festival poster.

"Charlotte," he asked, "what can you tell me about this festival everyone is talking about?"

"Oh, that's right! You are new here," she said with a smile. "I have not been for years, but it is quite an affair."

"How so?" he asked, hoping the conversation would lead naturally into his invitation of it to her and her mother.

"I suppose it shares some similarities with other large social events. There are food items and drinks for sale, along with some handcrafted items people have made. Once, I saw small carved boxes. Another person had knitted scarves. There is dancing and merriment, but our town—and perhaps it's silly, I've never heard of another doing it—but our town has an event for all of the unmarried individuals to participate in, if they'd like."

"What happens with that?" he asked, glancing at the festival poster again before looking back to her.

"Well, it's used as an excuse for young people to start courting or to spend a few moments with someone they are interested in. Years and years ago, when the town was first formed, there was a terrible snowstorm," she explained. "The town founder's daughter had been traveling and didn't return before the storm hit. So, men from all over set out in their sleighs to find her. One did, and they fell in love on their journey back to town. Her family was so grateful, they threw a large celebration for the man, and it ended with his proposal to her."

Justin frowned. Perhaps this was not something that she'd want to attend with him. It seemed to have romantic overtones, and they were, at this time, nothing more than friends. Still...it might not hurt to ask. Perhaps he would just see where the conversation led. Justin nodded as a reply. "I see."

She shrugged. "Almost everyone knows who they are going to have a sleigh ride with anyway. If they choose to have one. Some people simply sit and talk. The sleighs come from those who have brought them or loaned them for the event."

She laughed, and the sound was so beautiful to his ears. "When I was a girl, we used to take our sleigh out every winter. It was so much fun. It's sat neglected for a good number of years, but it's one thing we've kept, despite selling so many others. One day, Mother says we will fix it up."

"I've never been in one," Justin admitted.

"Oh, I do hope you get the chance. It's tremendous! It's like you are flying," Charlotte told him, excitement in her voice.

"I can imagine. Well, the festival sounds most interesting." He hesitated. "Are you...are you attending with anyone?"

"I hope to be," she said, blushing prettily.

His heart sped up. Was she thinking about him? Should he ask her? His stomach started to spin at the idea. It was a mix of nerves and excitement. How should he react if she said yes? His mind was whirling, and he was trying to force the words to his lips when she spoke again.

"A friend of mine told me someone had asked if I had a beau. I've not had the chance to speak with him, though, to see if he'd like to ask me to attend or ride with him."

"Ah, I see." Justin nodded, hoping he didn't display the disappointment he felt. Of course there was someone. A woman like her? There was likely more than one man with his eye on Charlotte. "What's his name?"

"August Middleton," Charlotte answered.

August Middleton. The name first sent a flash of anger through him, and then disgust. That's the man that Charlotte was interested in? It was no wonder the man was fascinated by her, but she was attracted to that arrogant man?

"I'll be doing a few things to set up in the examination room," Justin told Charlotte and turned, trying to hold in his anger.

Once in there, he left the door open, but moved to the far side of the room and closed his eyes, trying to focus on his breathing. The moment he'd met August Middleton, he'd despised the man. Charlotte was too good for him. She deserved someone kind. Even if it wasn't him. She deserved anyone but that man.

Eyes still closed, he recalled the day after he'd arrived. Only about two weeks ago, he remembered it clearly. The ground was muddy. It had rained the night before, and puddles had collected. Justin was on his horse, coming back from a short tour of the town's outskirts with Dr. Jeffers.

Their horses had pulled alongside the main street, and Justin had dismounted. The horse chose that moment to step forward, and Justin lost his footing, one boot landing rather splashily in the mud.

A man had been walking past, and the mud splattered on his pant leg. "I apologize," Justin had said instantly. "My horse—"

"Look what you've done!" the man snapped. "My clothes cost more than you make in a month. These boots, three months."

"I said I was sorry," Justin said, walking closer and remaining calm. "If you'd like me to, I'll cover the cleaning bill."

The man sneered at him. "You just moved here, didn't you? You don't know who I am, or you'd have been a lot more careful."

Dr. Jeffers had walked over, but the man ignored him, instead boisterously laughing. "My father owns most of this town, and a few hundred thousand acres along with more cattle than you can imagine. We can run out anyone we don't like—and I have before—so watch it. Better yet, keep out of my way."

August looked at him, his face darkening. "I don't like the look of you. Dressed all prissy, like you're better than anyone else. A fancy Yankee, aren't you? You get one warning. Next time, I might not be so nice."

The man strode off, and Justin had looked at Dr. Jeffers in surprise. "Who was that? And doesn't he realize the war has been over for a long time now?"

"August Middleton," the man said, his lips pressed together. "He likes to stir things up for fun. He'll choose someone to make an enemy out of for no good reason. Looks like he chose you. Luckily, I don't see a lot of him. When he started getting too big for his britches a few years ago, he wasn't punished. Acts just like his father. Luckily, their business takes them all over, so they aren't here a lot. Just come in every now and again to throw their weight around. And I suspect, to look for a wife now that it's about time. Especially with the festival approaching."

That was the first time he'd heard the festival mentioned, but he hadn't asked anything more, being so surprised still by the event. And now that he knew more about it, that it also involved some sort of courting activity...

Pain ripped through his chest. An ache of longing for Charlotte to be his. For her to look at him the same way she did at the memory of August Middleton.

Charlotte was at her desk now, he noticed as he peered into the office. She kept brushing her hair back impatiently. It was lovely. She was lovely. Why August?

His reaction was foolish, he knew. He and Charlotte hardly knew each other, but there was something in him that just knew. There was a pull, a force, something that whispered to his very soul that Charlotte was meant to be his.

But, of course, if she didn't feel that also, he wasn't going to force himself upon her. Couldn't. She didn't deserve to have attention paid to her if it wasn't welcome.

If only she would accept it. His heart ached for her to. To look at him with that same smile that came to her lips when she thought about August Middleton. To whisper his name the way she spoke August's.

He didn't quite know when it had happened, but he knew that he'd fallen head over heels for Charlotte.

A patient came in, and Justin forced himself to smile and greet her. But the entire time he was listening to Mrs. Donovan explain the pain in her shoulder, his thoughts kept drifting to Charlotte.

She was so incredible. Could have any man, any man at all...How could that one be the man she was interested in?

Chapter 7

Charlotte hummed to herself as she ran first her eyes and then her fingers over the collection of fabric. It was difficult to choose what she wanted. There was a beautiful deep green plaid, but there was a lovely maroon. A deep blue also spoke to her. It was a difficult decision.

The fabric for her mother had been an easy choice, as a few weeks back she'd seen her mother looking longingly at a beige color with faint gold stripes. It was much harder to decide for herself, as this would likely be the most important dress that she ever wore.

It might be the dress that won her August.

Charlotte turned to the thread. She'd made up her mind to get the green, and was looking for thread that blended in best, when she felt someone standing close to her. She glanced up, expecting to see the shop owner or his wife ready to measure her fabric. To her surprise, it was neither. It was August.

"Oh," she gasped. "You-you startled me."

"Making a new dress?" he asked, looking at the fabrics.

"Yes, for the festival," she answered, feeling shy. She'd hardly talked to August since they'd been in school, and that was years before. Until now, other than a hello here and there, she'd simply imagined him talking to her.

"I like the blue," he said, nodding to it. "Suits you."

"That's just the one I was getting," Charlotte said, smiling up at him.

August nodded. "A good choice. I'll be at the festival as well."

A heavy silence came between them. Charlotte swallowed. "Is that so? Planning to enjoy the afternoon? Or are you also planning to spend it in someone's company?"

She'd asked him. Charlotte could hardly believe she'd let the words come from her mouth.

His eyes filled with amusement. "I've got my eye on someone. If she'll be there and come up to me, I couldn't say."

Charlotte nodded, momentarily at a loss for words. She suddenly felt very hot, and it was difficult to breathe. Was he insinuating that he'd be interested in her? Had her friend Betty been truthful?

"Where have you been keeping yourself?" August asked. "I've not seen you around for a while."

"Oh." Charlotte's mind spun. Did that mean he'd been looking for her? "I got a job," she explained. "It keeps me quite busy."

"Where at?" he asked, picking up a nearby book, turning it over in his hands, and putting it back. Charlotte recalled he'd never been one for books.

"For the new doctor," she said. "I take care of his notes and patient charts, and assist a little if he needs me in some other way."

A sneer passed over his face. "That so? I met him. Don't care for the man."

"You don't?" Charlotte felt surprise, and it escaped in her voice. "Justin—Dr. Davis is very kind. He treats everyone nicely and fairly. I can't imagine what he did that upset you."

"You don't need to," he said. "That's men's business." He gave her a long, studying look. "Do I need to worry that you are planning to go for him at the festival?"

"N-no," Charlotte stammered. "Not at all. The doctor and I are merely friends. We work together. That's all."

"Huh. I see. Maybe I should form my own opinion on that," August said. Then, he gave her a wink. "After all, I have to figure out if I've got competition or not."

Her cheeks felt as though they were on fire. It was true! August did like her! She must be the one he hoped would go to him at the festival and ask for a sleigh ride. Her pulse was so rapid, Charlotte hoped she didn't faint. She could hardly believe what was happening.

"Well, I've got to go. See you around," August said, tipping his hat to her.

Charlotte watched as he strode out of the store, and let her eyes follow him for a moment. She felt almost giddy. She couldn't wait to tell her mother and start making her dress.

"Have you chosen?" the shop owner asked, coming up to her.

"Yes, the blue fabric," Charlotte said, "with some thread for it, please."

She waited almost impatiently for the length to be cut, folded, and wrapped. Finally, she took her bundle and hurried away.

Usually, the two miles home didn't feel that far, but today they did. Charlotte was anxious to start on her dress. She had to make it perfect.

When her house was just before her, since no one was around, Charlotte nearly ran to the front door and burst in.

"My goodness," her mother gasped from the kitchen. "Is everything all right?"

"It's more than all right," Charlotte said happily. "I was choosing my fabric for a dress, and you'll never guess who else was in the store."

"Hmm," her mother said teasingly. "Let me see..." She sliced another carrot and asked, "August Middleton?"

"Yes." Charlotte giggled. "I was going to get a different fabric, but he said he liked the blue, so I chose that." She unwrapped the bundle and pulled out the length of cloth.

"Oh, that is a lovely color, and I'm glad you chose it. However, it's important to choose what you like as well, not just what you hope someone will like you in." Her mother scooped the carrots into a simmering pot.

"Now, Mama, I know for a fact you wore lavender because Papa liked you in it, even though you got a bit tired of the color."

Her mother laughed. "Perhaps," she admitted. "As long as you are happy."

"I am," Charlotte said. "This was one of the three choices I was torn between."

She handed another wrapped bundle to her mother. "I bought you something as well."

"You shouldn't have," her mother said, worry on her face. "My dear, your pay is for you."

"And I chose to get this for you," Charlotte said, jutting out her chin stubbornly. "Go on, open it."

Her mother wiped her hands on her apron, then slowly unwrapped the brown paper. She gasped when she saw the fabric, and tears formed in her eyes. "My dear girl, you shouldn't have," she said as she stroked the fabric, sliding one finger down the faint stripe.

"I should have," Charlotte said, hugging her mother. "We shall each have a new dress, Mama. We deserve it. It has been too long since either of us has had that luxury."

Her mother didn't answer, but turned back to the stove, wiping at her eyes. Charlotte decided to change the subject.

"August did say something strange," she admitted.

It hadn't occurred to her at the time, but now it sank in. She frowned slightly as she recalled his words.

"What was that?" her mother asked curiously.

"He said he didn't care for Dr. Davis. Then, he asked me if I was going to choose him at the festival. The doctor, I mean." Charlotte shook her head. "Why do you think he asked that? And why do you think he doesn't care for the doctor?"

"Perhaps he is jealous." Her mother shrugged. "The doctor is a good man. He's very important to the community, and has taken the time to help a good number of people, just in his short time here."

"The Middletons are also important," Charlotte said. "Why, they own quite a bit of land, including in the town, and a large number of cattle. They provide a lot of jobs."

"They do," her mother agreed. "So there's no reason for August to feel unimportant. Perhaps it's just some sort of a pride thing. He could be thinking that he doesn't want the woman he's chosen to be looking at someone else."

"He doesn't need to worry about that," Charlotte laughed. "I've had my eye on August since we were in school together. I know almost every girl did. It's almost like a dream that he might be interested in me. He was hinting about hoping for a particular person to ask him for a sleigh ride."

Her mother smiled. "Well, if he is the one that you want, I hope you get to have him. You deserve nothing but happiness."

Her mother picked up the blue fabric and began to mumble to herself as Charlotte let her thoughts wander. Yes. Yes, she did want August, and more than anything, she hoped that on the day of the festival, when she walked up to him and took his arm, he'd smile down at her and go on that sleigh ride.

There was a knock at the door, and Charlotte stood. "I'll get it, Mama."

She was surprised when she'd opened the door to see the young boy who did general store deliveries. "For you," he said, thrusting a package at her. "Already got my tip."

As the boy ran off, Charlotte stared in surprise. Had she left something behind at the store? She walked back to the kitchen.

"Who was that?" her mother asked.

"A delivery boy. He brought a package."

"What's in it?" Her mother glanced over at the small bundle.

Charlotte shrugged and untied the twine around the package. A long, deep blue ribbon was revealed.

"Oh that's lovely," her mother said. "Did you forget to bring that home?"

"I didn't buy this," Charlotte said, wrinkling her nose. Then, she gasped. "It must have been August! This must be a gift from him!"

She spun around the kitchen. Tomorrow, she'd wear it in her hair, in case she saw him. Once the dress was finished, she'd add it here and there to it, unless she kept it for her hair. Charlotte couldn't remember ever being so happy.

Chapter 8

Justin rubbed at his eyes. He'd been up early, unable to sleep. All he could think about was Charlotte and August, together. Not for even a moment would he let himself listen to the little whisper in his mind that told him that he liked Charlotte. No, that voice got pushed away as far as he could get it.

It would be highly inappropriate, both to develop feelings for his employee, or to put her in a compromising position. It also might jeopardize her happiness. That's all he wanted, to see Charlotte happy, and smiling.

Even if that wasn't with him, as much as it pained him to say.

The door opened, and he heard her footsteps as she entered the office. He'd memorized the sound. He was a fool. Falling in love with a woman who would never look at him that way.

Justin sighed, then came out from the storage room, where he'd been checking his supplies.

"Good morning," he greeted her.

"Good morning," Charlotte answered. "Did I see you in the storage room? Do you need help with anything?"

"Yes, your help would be appreciated. I was starting a list of items that I need. I will either fetch them myself from Cottonwood Falls or send for them next week," he told her. "I don't like to get too low on supplies, especially in the winter."

"That makes a lot of sense," she agreed, and draped her shawl on her chair. As she unwound her scarf, he caught sight of a scrap of blue.

"That's a lovely ribbon you have in your hair," he said. She'd weaved it into a braid, and it looked quite beautiful.

"Thank you," she said, her cheeks turning bright red. "It was a gift. From August."

"From—" Justin stopped. From August? *From August*? It hadn't been. It had been from him! But fool that he was, he hadn't wanted to put his name on it. Hadn't wanted her to feel obligated or uncomfortable. So, of course she'd think it was from August.

He closed his eyes a moment, then opened them and forced cheerfulness into his voice. "The color suits you."

"Oh! What's this?" Charlotte asked. She held up a blue cushion that had been placed in her chair.

"Ah, well, you sit so much, I was hoping that would make your chair more comfortable," Justin said. "It is sturdy, but also rather hard."

He'd bought the cushion yesterday afternoon, the same time he'd bought the ribbon. Did she notice the colors matched?

"Thank you! I appreciate this so much," Charlotte said. "I can sit on it, or use it for my back. It was very thoughtful of you."

"It was my pleasure," Justin mumbled, and turned away. He tried to feel glad that at least she'd liked the gifts, but he stung too much, still hurt that she hadn't realized the ribbon was from him. He had hoped she'd have remembered.

Yesterday, she'd wished that she had something to tie her hair back with. True, she hadn't known he'd overheard her muttering to herself. But, he'd remembered, and knowing that he could make her life better with such a trifle, was more than happy to do so. A rich man he was not, but a pastry each day and a ribbon? That he could do.

But of course, she thought it was August. It was always August. He couldn't stand the man, and couldn't bear hearing his name over and over.

"Oh! Justin," Charlotte said suddenly.

"Yes?" he asked. His breath caught as he looked at her. Her eyes were so clear, her face filled with sweetness, despite her hardships. She needed someone to care for her, to treat her well. That was why he loathed the idea of her being with a despicable man like August Middleton.

Justin took a deep breath. He needed to stop thinking such thoughts. It wasn't right to feel anger and envy.

"Mama wouldn't admit it, but she seemed down in her spirits this morning. Would you mind stopping by to check on her?"

"Of course," he said. "Actually..." Justin walked over and looked at the schedule. "I thought so. Just before lunch, we've no patients. Would you be able to manage here while I went then? I'll ride and be back before our patients after lunch."

"Oh, yes! That would make me feel so much better," Charlotte said, sagging in relief. "Thank you."

Anything more they might have said was saved for later, as the first patient arrived. Justin went about his morning, and tried to ignore the ache that filled him. He'd never been in love before, but he'd seen how it affected others. However, instead of the joy and happiness and light mood, like Charlotte had when she thought about August, he had the blackness, the aching heart. Unrequited love, a novel might say.

The morning dragged on, and it was a welcome relief for him to step outside of his office, bag in hand, and head toward Charlotte's home. As usual, she had worked hard in the office that morning. She was an incredible help. However, also as usual, her eyes would seek through the window toward the festival poster. Or perhaps they sought August.

Justin couldn't wait until this festival was over.

But the thought made his step falter. When it was...what then? Would Charlotte be courting? Engaged? Have a date to marry the man he knew was all wrong for her? She couldn't see that, though he wished she did.

He moved faster toward his horse. Because he was cold, he told himself. Not because he was trying to outpace those thoughts constantly tormenting him.

After a time, the Harrison place appeared through the trees, and he went up the worn steps. He knocked, then let his eyes take in the large home. It must have been fine back in its day. It looked to be four or five bedrooms at least. Though he'd not seen much beyond the kitchen on his previous visit, he was sure the home had brought pleasure to the Harrisons.

The door swung open just then. "Mrs. Harrison." He smiled. "Charlotte told me you were not feeling well."

"Oh," the older woman faltered. She shook her head and then shrugged. "Come in, Dr. Davis." She stepped back, then asked, "Join me in the kitchen for some tea?"

As he followed her into the warmth of the kitchen, she bustled about and soon brought over two steaming cups.

"Thank you," he said, wrapping his fingers around one of them. "Just when I think it can't get any colder outside, it surprises me."

Mrs. Harrison laughed. It didn't quite meet her eyes. "You are quite right," she agreed.

"Now then," Justin said, setting down his cup and looking at her carefully. "Tell me, how are you? You don't appear to be in ill health, but I can tell something isn't quite right."

"No, my health is fine. Though, perhaps I should say my physical health is not the problem. My emotions are distressed, that is all, and no need to worry." She gave a soft sigh and shook her head. "It's hard at times not to feel sorry for one's self in the circumstances life sees fit to give you."

Justin nodded. "I understand what you mean. I've been feeling that way myself as of late. Perhaps it's the weather. Cloudy skies lead to cloudy moods."

Charlotte's mother nodded. "Indeed. It has been rather overcast. It's also likely the festival talk that has me feeling down. These moods will pass. They always do. It's difficult at times to see others enjoying themselves, carefree, when your own worries cluster about you."

Her words were said not with self pity, but a practicality he understood. In fact, he couldn't have said them any better himself.

"This festival." Justin tried not to grind out his words, though he felt the bad taste in his mouth at them. "That's all anyone seems to talk about. The young women of this town seem near half out of their senses, the young men the same. There's more giggling than talking. Even in my older patients."

Mrs. Harrison laughed again, but this time her face lit up. "Yes, I suppose the tradition might seem odd to you, but it is the bright spot for the young folks. It's a chance for them to declare in front of the town the person they choose to spend time with. Of course, there are many courtships that take place at other times, but the young folk enjoy dressing up in their finery, strolling through the town and sampling the food and beverages, looking at the things for sale and just enjoying the day. It's a nice social event for all, and helps to ease the stretch between Christmas and spring, where there is little ahead but dreariness and cold weather."

Justin rubbed at his eyes. "Just the same, I will be glad when it's over," he told her.

Mrs. Harrison's considering gaze, filled with warmth and understanding, filled him with something he realized he missed dearly. The chance to confide in someone. Being so far from his family, and not having made any friends just yet, left him with more burdens than he had shoulders for, at times.

"Tell me, Doctor," she said. "What has you so distraught?"

The temptation to tell of his adoration for Charlotte, and his desire to know her better, weighed heavily upon him. He longed to tell her how he despised the man Charlotte set her gaze on. To explain how his heart ached from the fact the object of his affection didn't even notice him, though she was all he could think about.

But Justin merely smiled, made sure his features were composed, and reassured her. "It's just a bit of winter melancholy."

Chapter 9

"Goodbye! I'll see you tomorrow," Charlotte called as she shut the doctor's office door behind her. It was a mere five days before the festival, and she needed to hurry. Her dress wasn't quite finished. Hopefully tonight she'd make progress on it.

As she did each time she walked through the town, Charlotte peered about for August. She tried to do it discreetly, but she looked just the same, always hoping to see a flash of him. Even better would be a moment to talk with him.

Disappointment flooded her as she passed the sheriff's office, the bakery, and the diner. There had been no sight of him. It wasn't much further and all the buildings of the town would be gone, and she'd have the lonely walk home.

"Charlotte!"

She froze at the sound of her name. Hesitantly, she turned around, and her eyes widened. It was August!

"H-hello," she said, feeling suddenly shy.

"The festival is in a few days," he said, by way of greeting.

He smiled, and then stared at her in a frank way that actually made Charlotte feel uncomfortable. He'd never done that before—not that she was aware of—but just now, his eyes seemed to start at the top of her head, then slowly move down, lingering in places she didn't care for. She pretended she didn't notice, and hoped no one else did.

"Yes, it is," she answered, trying to ignore the distaste that had filled her. Why was August looking at her like that?

"I can't wait to see you in that blue dress," he continued. "You'll be the prettiest one there."

Her cheeks colored, and she wasn't quite sure what to say. Charlotte felt confused. One moment, he made her feel awkward, as though she wanted to hide. The next, he was making her feel flattered. Was the first acceptable, if they might end up courting? She wasn't sure, and struggled with the idea.

Fat flakes of snow fell, but August didn't say goodbye, and Charlotte didn't want to just leave, even if she was starting to shiver.

"So, you are still working for the doctor, huh? I'd have thought he'd have run you off by now." August crossed his arms and scowled in the direction of the doctor's office. "I don't like that man. Thinks he's better than anyone else."

"Doctor Davis? He doesn't think that at all. He's so nice," Charlotte started, then faltered as August gave her a look that pierced her chest. A strange feeling formed in her stomach at his glare. August seemed...angry? And she wasn't sure if it was at her.

Charlotte bit her lip. She didn't want to upset him. But what he said about Justin simply wasn't true.

Leaning forward, August dropped his voice. "He's not. It's just an act. For his patients," he told her confidently. "Besides, I have to admit, Charlotte. Maybe this is the real reason I don't care for him. I don't know if I like you working there. You, alone with the doctor? That puts you in a compromising position. I can't consider a woman who is questionable. He's wrong and inconsiderate to do that to you."

He smirked, "I'm surprised your mother approved it. What kind of woman would let her daughter be placed in that sort of situation? Unless she's hoping for a wedding?"

Charlotte didn't know if she should panic or be angry. How could he say such things? About her mother! And about the doctor! There was nothing, nothing at all, inappropriate about their relationship. In fact, he had been nothing but considerate and conscientious about appearances.

The curtains were always kept open, her desk was far from his, they were never in one of the smaller rooms together without a patient there, and she couldn't imagine Justin being the sort to ever take advantage of someone, let alone a woman. She and her mother needed that income. Desperately needed it. Because of the doctor's kindness, things weren't so dire for them.

She had just opened her mouth to tell him so when the doctor rode up in his wagon. A wool blanket was across his lap, and his bag was in the seat next to him.

"Hello," he said. "I thought that was you. Charlotte, I've got to visit a patient on the outskirts of town. Would you like a ride home? It's on my way."

Her feet felt frozen to the ground in her worn shoes. The idea was appealing. She was about to accept the offer, but August's glare—first at her and then the doctor—made Charlotte tense, then shake her head and lower her eyes. "No, thank you. I enjoy the walk home after sitting so much."

Justin nodded, but when she glanced at him, she could tell he wasn't convinced. She gave him a small smile. With a long look, as though he were making sure she was well enough to walk home, he nodded once more and then continued on his way.

It was getting colder, and the wind had picked up. The cool stare August was giving her wasn't helping with her shivers. "You made the right choice," he told her, then spit on the ground. The act repulsed her. When had he become so impolite? "You know, once we marry, you won't need to work. No, you can just stay home all day. Tend to the house's needs. My needs."

August turned then and walked away without another word. He left Charlotte standing there, shocked and...if she were to let herself admit it, a little scared. The August she'd just seen was so different from the one she thought she knew.

He'd mentioned marriage. That should have made her feel happy. So, why didn't it? Even though they'd spoken for so long, it felt as though everything Charlotte thought she had known about him was very, very different.

Charlotte's nearly numb feet carried her home. Her mind was troubled, and she hoped her mother wouldn't notice. She didn't want to worry her, but suddenly, she wasn't looking forward to the festival. A marriage to August was what she thought she had wanted. Had dreamed of. However, suddenly, he was so cold. So angry, and filled with suspicion about her actions. He had even insinuated that she might be seen as compromised.

Hot, angry tears burned in Charlotte's eyes, but she didn't let them fall. She'd given up tears long ago.

The sun was nearly to bed by the time Charlotte approached her house, and she yawned, weary from the long day at work, the confusing and troubling conversation with August, and the walk.

It was a bright spot, however, that today was the day she was paid. It felt good to be contributing to the household finances. Her mother had finally agreed to it, as long as Charlotte kept a third of her wages for herself. They'd soon have a small nest egg and could begin to purchase much needed items, and perhaps do a few repairs to their home. She had so many things she wanted to surprise her mother with.

"I'm here," Charlotte called as she walked inside and hung up her thick shawl. Her mother had insisted she have a better one, since she was walking back and forth each day. With the frigid air, she was more than grateful for it.

Justin had offered to pick her up in the mornings, but he already did so much for her, like getting her something from the bakery each day, Charlotte didn't want to take advantage of his kindness. It would mean so much more work for him. And after the incident this afternoon when he'd offered to take her home, she knew she'd made the right decision. She didn't want August to see her with the doctor and assume that she wasn't interested in him.

But...was she? Should she still be? It was clear that he was interested in her, but Charlotte felt unsettled each time she thought about how he'd looked at her today, as though she were a meal he wanted to devour, and how he'd spoken to her, as if she were so far beneath him. She physically felt sick at the words he'd said about her mother. One of the most honest and caring people who existed. Her mother never once, in all the years she'd been eligible, pushed her to marry for her mother's sake.

If August was interested in her, why was he treating her that way?

Another worry crossed her mind about what might happen if she accepted a ride in the doctor's wagon. August, if he was angry enough, might tell others that her reputation was questionable. Then, the doctor would be forced to let her go. Perhaps he'd even have to leave town. No, she didn't dare risk her situation or his. He was too good of a man to deserve that.

During dinner, Charlotte was quiet. When her mother asked, she explained she was tired.

With an understanding nod, her mother carried the conversation for them. Charlotte only half listened. Her mind was too worried. Had she made a mistake, encouraged August to think something she didn't mean for him to? Was that what had happened this afternoon? She replayed every interaction they'd had in her mind. No. She had no idea why he behaved that way.

"I began making lace again, now that we've had a little money to buy what I need," her mother said, holding up a strip of the decorative white trim, and bringing Charlotte out of her thoughts.

"Oh, that's wonderful," Charlotte said as she took it and examined the pattern. Her mother was a fine lace maker. "You've always made the most beautiful of pieces."

"I think I will go into town in the morning, perhaps when you leave? I will stop by the general store and show some small pieces and see if they'd be interested in buying some of them. I could make something larger, as well. It would help our income."

"I bet they would," Charlotte said. "Be sure to stop in at the dressmaker as well. You make lovely cuffs and collars in addition to your hankies and doilies."

"That's a good idea," her mother agreed. She looked at Charlotte for a long moment and smiled. "It's so good to see you happy, my dear. It seems that things have improved so much over the last month."

Charlotte nodded. "They have," she said. "I am grateful for my job, and I enjoy it. It makes me feel content to help others."

"You have always had the instinct to nurture," her mother agreed. She hesitated. "I think that means you will also make a fine wife one day. When I go to town tomorrow, I wonder if I will run into the young man you have set your eye upon. It's been a while since I've seen young Mr. Middleton. Perhaps I was mistaken in my earlier sentiments, and he has become thoughtful and ready to settle down."

"I told you," Charlotte said lightly.

But what she hadn't told her mother, she thought to herself that night as she tossed and turned in bed, was that perhaps her mother hadn't been wrong in her original assessment of August.

Was it too late to withdraw her affections? It might be. And if she did, what would happen to her mother? Her health was fragile, and she depended on Charlotte to help care for her. It was a task Charlotte took upon herself willingly, but it would be much easier if she were a woman of means. Then, she could give her mother all she needed. The Middletons might provide those means.

Winning August's attention, and ultimately his affection, had seemed like the right path several weeks ago. After all, she'd been mooning over him for years. But the more she spoke to him, the less she liked how he acted.

Her mother's words from a long-ago conversation chose that exact moment to float through her mind.

"My dear, seeking a match only for a better financial situation isn't a good idea. You need to find someone you can love and who loves you."

Charlotte's lips trembled, but she shook her head, turned over determinedly, and pulled her quilt to her chin. "It's too late," she said, her voice firm. "I've set my course, and now I must follow it."

It didn't matter if doubt filled her. If she couldn't win August Middleton for herself, she would likely be alone for the rest of her life. There was no one else who cared for her, and she desperately, urgently wanted both love and a better future.

As soon as the thought came, Charlotte stilled, then shook her head. No, that wasn't true. There were others, like the doctor, who cared for her. But only as a friend. August might be her only opportunity for a chance at happiness.

Chapter 10

It was unusually beautiful outside. No patients had come in that mid-morning, and Justin took advantage of the lull to go for a short walk around the town. He was just on his way back when he spotted Charlotte's mother walking in the direction of her home. Her jaw was set, her shoulders square, and her pace frantic. It was obvious something was wrong.

"Mrs. Harrison," he called as he caught up to her. "Stop a moment."

She did, and turned a face filled with anguish toward him. "Doctor," she said quietly as she fought to smooth over her features.

"What happened?" he demanded. "I can tell something has. Let me help you." His head twisted side to side, seeking the source of her upset.

Mrs. Harrison paced a few steps away, and then back. "I cannot tell you," she answered, her voice tense.

"And I cannot let you leave in this condition," he replied, gently taking her elbow and leading her over to a bench just a short distance away. "Something is wrong, and I would be remiss as your doctor and as your friend if I let you go and something happened to you."

She was quiet for a long moment, then met his eyes. "Doctor, can I count on your discretion?"

"Of course," he answered. He looked down at her hands. They were trembling. Concern filled him, and he reached over to check her pulse. It was rapid. It was obvious she was agitated, and it wasn't good for her to be. Mrs. Harrison had been through so much in recent years, yet hadn't seemed to let it bother her. This must be incredibly serious for it to have shaken her this much.

"Very well," she relented. "I had gone into the dressmaker's shop to show some samples of lace I'd made. They liked them and wanted to buy more. I thought to stop over at your office and let Charlotte know. However, when I was leaving, just outside of the building I overheard a man laughing about all of the young women after him, and how he'd have his pick before the festival."

She took a deep breath. "That isn't uncommon. Some young men, women too, let their egos take over when the festival comes around. I wasn't intending to eavesdrop, but the conversation was right there. There was no way to avoid them."

"I understand," Justin assured her.

"I hadn't looked to see who was speaking yet," she continued. "But then, one of the men said that he was leading on three women, one being Charlotte. I glanced over then, and saw it was August Middleton. I was so angry that I took leave of my senses. All I could think about was how hurt she'd be when she found out. Especially if she was not the one he chose at the end."

Justin closed his eyes a moment. He could imagine the scene. And August's reaction. "What happened next?" he asked, almost afraid to know.

Mrs. Harrison's whole body trembled, and he took her hands into his. "Take some deep breaths," he told her. "Slowly. There you go."

"I-I told him that I thought what he was doing was terrible. I'm not sure if he recognized me. He pushed past me and laughed, then wandered over to your office." She shook her head. "I assumed he went inside."

Justin glanced toward his practice. There, standing before the door was August, talking to Charlotte who was smiling at him. Anger filled him. It was all he could do to keep it in check as he turned to Charlotte's mother.

"Are you hurt?" he asked her.

"No," she said as she shook her head. "Not physically. But, Doctor, you must keep this between us. It would hurt Charlotte so to know that August wasn't completely interested in her."

She opened her mouth, then closed it. The worry on her face fueled his anger. "I won't say a word," he promised.

"I...I don't feel, in my heart, that August would ever choose Charlotte. We have nothing. He wants a woman to be a full package, beautiful and wealthy, he said. His father won't let him have anything else. It will devastate Charlotte when she learns that."

"If he loved her, none of that would matter," Justin said. He was grateful there weren't many people around. He knew he looked angry, and his eyes were likely smoldering. It was a struggle to have some semblance of calm in his voice.

What he wanted, right now, was to tell August he was a fool. That he didn't deserve Charlotte's affection. Wasn't worthy to even walk on the same street as her.

It was true, what Mrs. Harrison said. There were many people who would choose the one they married only to make themselves look better through their looks or their wealth.

That had never been something he'd thought of. He would take Charlotte no matter what. Even if she had nothing. He would give her everything that she wanted, if he could. If she'd just look at him the way he longed for her to.

"I feel responsible," Mrs. Harrison murmured. "If I had just tried harder, begged my husband not to sign those papers, perhaps we wouldn't be so badly off. Charlotte might have stood a better chance at a successful marriage if we had something, if she was better off."

"A marriage to that man isn't what she needs," Justin said, not caring if his voice sounded harsh. "What Charlotte needs is someone who loves her, thinks only of her. She is a woman worthy of far more than August Middleton. The fact that he can't see that, can't see beyond her beauty and cares about her monetary value shows what a fool he is."

He froze then. He'd said it aloud. Said too much. And to her mother! A surge of panic filled him, and he dared to glance at Mrs. Harrison. She was looking at him oddly, but then a soft smile came over her face.

"I-I must go," he said, rising quickly from the bench. "If-if you are well, then I will take my leave. You have my confidence, of course," he added.

"Thank you, Doctor," she said, still smiling. "Yes, I am well. But, one more thing."

"What is that?" he asked as she lightly placed her hand upon his arm.

"Consider telling her that you are attracted to her," she answered. "I would much rather have you become part of our family than August."

Justin blushed, then he shook his head as a bitter laugh broke forth. "Mrs. Harrison. I am keeping your confidence, so you must keep mine. Charlotte has no interest in me. Her happiness is all I want. Even if that's not with me."

He walked away then, knowing his shoulders were slumped. It was impossible not to feel conflicted. August was no longer in his doorway. For that he was glad. But a tightness had filled his chest, making it difficult to breathe. He knew that August wasn't a good person, but to hear a confirmation that he was merely leading Charlotte along felt almost more than he could bear.

A part of him was glad, to be sure. He knew what a despicable human the man was. But Charlotte didn't. She was in love with him. Longed for him. He made her happy.

Mrs. Harrison was right in that when Charlotte found out, if she found out, it would hurt her in the most terrible of ways. Justin knew that if she did marry August, it wouldn't be long before Charlotte learned how little she meant to him. It was apparent August was that sort of person.

Her mother's words came to him, and he entertained the thought, only for a moment, of telling her that he cared for her. But that would confuse her. Complicate things. He didn't want to risk losing her. Making her feel uncomfortable.

Oh, he could get by without a nurse, if he had to. But her friendship wasn't something he wanted to lose. Nothing was worth that. Their easy conversations, the way they would joke together—those things were valuable to him. Priceless, really.

Perhaps there was another way. He didn't need to be direct. Why, he'd simply hint that someone else might make her happier. Plant a little seed in her mind. Maybe that would open her eyes to the fact that there was someone better—much better—suited than August Middleton to be the man who received her love.

Chapter 11

Charlotte had just finished dusting and picked up the broom to sweep the front room when the doctor returned. She greeted him, then her smile faded. He looked upset. Was he unhappy? She couldn't tell, but there was a strange feeling about him.

He looked at her when she spoke, but it was as if his eyes didn't see her. Chills came over Charlotte, and she wondered what had happened in the short time that he'd been out.

"Justin?" she asked softly. "Are you all right?"

He shook himself and nodded. "Yes. Yes, of course. I just...there were some things on my mind. That is all."

She nodded and set the broom down, stepping closer. Her eyes scanned him once more. His eyes were tight, as were the corners of his mouth. He was a little flushed, and his knuckles were white from where he clenched his fists.

She wasn't sure if she should say anything, but couldn't stop herself. "You...aren't alright," she said softly. "I can tell. Can I help in any way? You are always taking care of others, but there is no one to take care of you. Let me do that. Please?"

He didn't answer, but stepped closer. His face softened, and he reached for her hands, which she willingly gave.

"Please?" she whispered again. "Tell me what has happened."

"Charlotte," he said, his voice almost inaudible.

He shook his head and started to pull away, but she tightened her grip on his hands. She could have sworn that his gaze focused for a moment on her lips.

When Justin met her eyes again, she saw conflicting emotions. Worry, fear, anger, hurt. It made her ache inside. It wasn't directed toward her, she knew this—but who? Who had done something so terrible that he was suffering so? A thought came to her then. He was a doctor. Sometimes, patients didn't recover. Was that what had happened just now? Had he lost a patient? He was such a caring man, he felt things deeper than he usually let on. Was this an instance where so much pain filled him that he leaked out?

"Charlotte," he said again, and his voice cracked.

"You can tell me," she promised. "I'm here for you."

Somehow, they'd moved close, so close they were mere inches away. If someone had walked in just then, they would have mistaken the two of them for being in a compromising position.

A heavy weight settled in the room. It felt nearly suffocating. The pressure filled Charlotte's chest, pushed against her throat, and she struggled to breathe.

"Did you ever think," Justin finally said, his eyes boring into her, "that perhaps what you thought you wanted wasn't what you needed? That it wasn't the right thing for you? And that something else, something better was also waiting...you just didn't know it?"

His words confused her. What was he talking about? It was almost as though he knew about her worries over August. She couldn't answer for that dreadful tightness and shook her head slightly.

"Or have you ever experienced happiness, complete and utter bliss right there...just within your grasp, but you didn't dare reach for it? Knew you couldn't? It didn't belong to you?" He closed his eyes for a moment, and when he opened them, such pain registered upon his face that Charlotte felt tears springing to her eyes.

"Charlotte," he whispered. "I want to tell you..."

"Tell me what?" she whispered when he didn't continue.

He swallowed visibly and moved almost impossibly closer. "Tell you that—"

A scream filled their ears. Startled, both backed away, the spell in the room broken. Outside, shouts and cries of terror filled the air, and Justin raced to the door, Charlotte right behind him.

The streets were chaos. Charlotte scanned the area and watched as people ran from all directions to a child lying in the street.

"It was a loose horse," a man told the sheriff, who had kneeled down next to the doctor. "Just caught it and took it to the stable. Broke loose and got spooked."

Charlotte hurried over. "Do you want your bag?" she asked, surprised at the calmness in her voice.

"Yes," Justin answered. "I don't know if we can move him, yet."

In a moment she was back, his heavy doctor's bag in her hand. She placed it next to him on the ground. Charlotte bent down and looked at the child, who was only about six years old. One arm was in a grotesque position, and his left leg was at an awkward angle. The child's eyes were closed.

"Who does he belong to?" Justin asked.

"Butcher's lad," the blacksmith said. "Already sent my boy to tell him."

The words were hardly out of his mouth before the butcher raced up the street and fell to his knees. "My boy! Doctor, can you help him?"

Justin didn't answer at first. He'd been running his fingers over the boy's body. He listened to his heart, checked the child's pulse, and then sat back on his heels. "Yes. I think he will be fine. Other than the obviously broken arm and leg. I don't see an injury to his head. I think the horse knocked him out of the way as he ran past, and that's how he ended up here. Quite possibly he is unconscious from the pain."

Justin looked for her and said, "Charlotte, we will move him to his house, but I think I need to bind his limbs to prevent more injury as we do. Can you return to the office and get me a canvas to move him on and strips of cloth? Afterward, I'll need you to bring me the standard items that we use for broken limbs. Can you do that?"

"Of course," Charlotte said, already rushing back to the doctor's office. She grabbed the canvas and cloth, then returned, seeking the large basket she knew was in the supply room.

Charlotte filled it with several medicines and ointments, clean bandages, strips of cloth, several of the tools she'd seen the doctor use and knew were not in his bag, and then lugged the heavy basket out of the office.

The street was still filled with people, and the sheriff saw her struggling and grabbed the basket. "Let me help you," he said. "I'll lead the way to their home."

"Thank you, Sheriff Steele," Charlotte said, hurrying next to him.

When they arrived, the house was in a state of almost calm. Charlotte wondered at how the doctor always seemed to project that when he was working. It was soothing for the patient. Had she not been with him moments before to see the absolute anguish upon his face and in his eyes, she'd have never thought he'd been struggling with anything in his life.

"Thank you," he said, reaching for the basket the sheriff had relinquished to her.

Their hands met, and Charlotte felt a small shock. If the doctor had felt it, he showed no sign.

"Mr. and Mrs. Hunter," Justin said, "Would you be so kind as to wait outside? Charlotte and I will tend to your boy, and I'll then speak with you in a few moments when we are done."

Mrs. Hunter nodded, still twisting her hands around, and left, murmuring something about making tea. Mr. Hunter followed her out and shut the door behind him.

Justin let out a soft sigh of relief. His face was focused, and Charlotte knew that all of his attention was on the young boy before him. She also knew in times like these, loved ones could be a distraction, especially in such a small space, and he needed room to work and concentrate.

"He was waking up as we brought him here," he told her, "and once I made sure there was no concussion, I gave laudanum to make him sleep. Should he wake while we set the bones, give him a few drops more. Only a few drops."

She nodded.

The doctor worked patiently, carefully. Charlotte assisted in cutting away the boy's shirt and pants to allow access to his wounded limbs. They worked in silence, and at least a half hour had passed. Painstakingly, Justin worked, hunched over and sweat beading on his brow. Charlotte observed how gentle he was in his ministrations, his long fingers deft in their movements.

Those same fingers that had wrapped around hers just an hour before.

The idea came from nowhere, and internally, she jolted. How was it that the reminder sent a tiny spark of lightning through her?

Another thought came just as quickly. Why was it that August did not? Did that mean something?

"Hand me that strip of cloth," Justin said.

She did as he asked. They were nearly finished. Justin wound the bandage, then reached into his bag for a small bottle which he set near the bed. He leaned back, sitting into a chair, and rested his head in his hands. He looked exhausted. Though he never spoke of it, Charlotte knew there was a great deal of exertion, mentally and physically, when dealing with severe injuries.

Charlotte covered the child with a quilt. When she straightened, Justin was standing. He gave her a warm smile. "You were a tremendous help. Thank you."

She wanted to say more. Wanted to reach out and touch him, but it wasn't proper to do so. They were in someone's home, there was a patient nearby, and she had no indication that he would even welcome that. So, she simply nodded.

"Let me collect your things while you speak with the Hunters," she said instead.

He nodded and went to the door, but Charlotte didn't miss the brush of his hand against her lower back, nor the tingles that it left.

Charlotte gathered his medical supplies, and then clutched his bag, closing her eyes for a moment. Had she not been so sure it was an accident, a mere brush from the small space and how near they were to each other, she'd have wondered if what he'd been wanting to tell her earlier had anything to do with an attraction toward her.

It was foolish. She knew it was. The doctor was kind to everyone. It was his job. His natural manner. It didn't mean that he found her attractive or liked her beyond friendship.

The doctor had endless redeeming qualities, and she enjoyed being around him and the effortless way they spoke. She was letting her hesitation about August muddle her feelings, that was all.

As they left the Hunters and walked down the street in silence, Charlotte glanced at Justin beneath her lashes. He looked tired, but at ease. They traded smiles when he glanced at her. For some reason she couldn't understand, her cheeks pinked.

As they approached the office, he opened the door for her. "I'll make us some tea," she offered. "You are more than deserving of a break."

Charlotte climbed the back stairs to Justin's private rooms and set about at his little stove. She enjoyed being here. But while the water heated, a devastating thought came to her.

When she was married to August, she'd never have these moments with Justin again. No treating patients, no anticipating his needs before he spoke of them, not even moments where she'd make tea and they'd simply sit and talk.

A terrible emptiness filled her at the idea.

Chapter 12

Justin hurried out of his office. It had been a long day, but while he'd hovered over the young Hunter boy, Charlotte and her distracting and delightful presence at his elbow, a thought had come to mind, and he was anxious to ask the sheriff his opinion on it.

For nearly an hour he had mulled over his decision, but he had finally decided it was the best course of action. His desire to help Charlotte and her mother in their dire situation far outweighed any discomfort on his part.

He walked to the sheriff's office and then stood outside the door, frowning. He was here, but what now? Did one knock at the door of a sheriff's office? Simply walk inside? He really wasn't sure. Until now, he'd never had a reason to stop by one.

Hesitating, Justin raised his hand to knock when the door opened and a woman came out.

"Oh, my goodness, excuse me," she said as she stopped, her nose a mere inch from his knuckles that had been prepared to rap upon the wooden door.

"My mistake, pardon me," Justin said. "I was coming to speak with the sheriff."

"He's at his desk. Come in. There's no need to wait outside," she told him, turning back the way she'd come from.

Justin followed her in a few steps, feeling a little nervous. He'd never been inside of the sheriff's office. There was a jail cell, two desks, a door leading somewhere—

"Asher, the new doctor was outside. I am afraid I nearly ran him over," the woman said apologetically.

"Forgive me," Justin said, "I was the one in the way. But I've not made your acquaintance yet, and you know me."

"I'm Isabelle," she said with a smile.

"My wife," the sheriff added as he dropped a kiss on her cheek. "See you in a while," he told her.

Isabelle nodded and left. Justin glanced around again, then back to the sheriff. "I wondered if I might have a word with you."

"Of course," Sheriff Steele said.

The door opened, and in walked the deputy. "Doctor," Jeff said by way of greeting.

"Deputy," Justin answered. "I'm glad you are here as well. What I have to ask is for both of your ears."

"Well then, let's take a seat," the sheriff said, and sat behind his desk.

He motioned to a chair, and Justin sat as well. He took a deep breath and tapped his foot. Jeff pulled a chair over. Justin felt their eyes on him and finally said, "This might be a bad idea, I don't know. That's why I came to you for your opinion."

The sheriff nodded slowly. Justin had heard the sheriff was a good man. He was fair and just, and he kept trouble out of the town. He'd even rescued his wife, Isabelle, from danger before they'd married. If anyone knew how to help, surely it would be him.

"You see," Justin said, "There's a family that was swindled out of just about everything they had years ago."

Jeff spoke, "That would be the Harrisons, correct?"

The sheriff frowned. "That was before I came, but I've heard a little about it. Mr. Harrison had a partner, didn't he? That who took advantage of him?"

"That's right," Justin said. "They've been in dire straits ever since."

"It's true," Jeff said. "That's why I'm sure Charlotte is pleased you hired her."

"What I'm wondering," Justin asked, "is if there is any way to prove that the partner swindled them. Perhaps legally regain at least some of what was once theirs."

The sheriff sighed and leaned back into his chair. "It's a good idea, really it is. But a lot of time has passed, and legally, if Mr. Harrison signed things over to his partner, then it's unlikely that will happen. You'd have to have a good, solid case for it. Do you know if there is any physical evidence? Threatening letters, perhaps? Witnesses?"

Justin shook his head. "Not that I know of. I'll ask Mrs. Harrison. I'd really like to help her if I can. She's a wonderful woman, and so is her daughter."

He stopped suddenly then, and froze. The sheriff was fighting back a smile. The deputy hadn't seemed to notice and was nodding vigorously. "Sure is. Her husband was a good man too."

"Why don't you see what you can find out, and then come back by?" Sheriff Steele suggested. He stood and walked Justin to the door. "Just come in next time. No need to knock. Treat this as any place of business."

Justin nodded. "Thank you. I will."

He hurried away before he could see that smirk the sheriff had. Internally, he was groaning. How could he have said that about Charlotte? What if word got around that the doctor was attracted to his assistant? Never mind if it was the truth or a lie. It wasn't the sort of thing he wanted going around.

He headed to the livery to get his horse, then stopped. The general store was right there. Why not get Charlotte a box of sweets, as a thank you for all she'd done today?

Pushing open the door, Justin browsed for a moment, then selected a tin of hard candies. He wasn't sure what she liked, but most people liked these, didn't they? Justin paid, got his horse, and headed to the Harrison home, hoping that he wouldn't be intruding.

Once there, he started up the porch to knock, but Mrs. Harrison opened it before he could. "Doctor," she greeted. "What brings you here?"

"I wanted to speak with you for a few moments," he said. "And to apologize if I've butted into your business unwanted."

She raised a brow at him, and Justin leaned forward to whisper, "Not *that* business."

"Ah. Do come in. Dinner is almost ready. Please say you will stay." She led him through the house.

"Only if it's no trouble," he said.

"Not a bit." She smiled. "I made a lovely potato soup. There's too much for just Charlotte and myself."

Just then, Charlotte came in. "I thought I heard you," she said. "Hello."

"Hello," he answered. "I—oh, these are for you." He held out the box of sweets.

Charlotte took it, a delighted expression upon her face. "Oh! Thank you. Did August leave these for me? He said he had a surprise for me."

Justin's breath stuck, and a rock seemed to land heavily in his stomach. "I-er—" Words wouldn't come. Wouldn't form. How could she have thought those were from August? If he said something now, it would either make him look a liar, or August.

Mrs. Harrison met his eye. She raised her brows, inviting him to say something, but he shook his head.

"Mrs. Harrison," he said, "I'm afraid I can't stay, I've an urgent appointment, but I wanted to have a few moments to talk with you, if I may?"

"Of course," she said.

They sat at the kitchen table. Her expression was one of sympathy, and he tried to ignore it. He couldn't bear her pity. "I visited the sheriff," he said, jumping into things. "I asked him about what had happened with your husband. If there was anything that could be done, even years later."

She sighed and shook her head. "I do doubt it, Doctor, though you are very kind to worry about us."

"He said that if you had any evidence, letters that were threatening, something like that, he might be able to help more," Justin said.

"If that were the case, I'd gladly give you what I had, but no. The man was silver tongued. He spoke with flattering and honeyed words. He was good at what he did, and by the time it was discovered, it was too late." She dropped her gaze, then met his eyes once more. "It all happened so quickly, it seems, and there was nothing suspect."

Justin heaved a sigh. "I understand. I will still make inquiries, if you have no objection?"

"I don't," she said, and stood when he did. "Are you sure you can't stay?"

"I cannot," he whispered.

Her understanding look was her reply, and Justin left.

On the ride back, he thought about how he was a fool. How, even if he did manage to help the Harrisons, that might make Charlotte even more attractive to August. But it didn't matter. It was the right thing to do, and he at least wanted to try.

He returned his horse and started back to his office. The sky was growing dim. All he wanted to do was to climb into bed and read. He had to have something on his shelf to take his mind off of his anger at August, and his longing for Charlotte.

It was a dangerous thing being a doctor. The temptation was there to use this medicine or that one to numb his tortured mind, but he didn't dare. One step in that direction might take him down a path of no return. It had been one of the first lessons in medical school, and something he'd witnessed firsthand while in school.

No, there were other ways to cope, even if they might not lead him to oblivion.

"Doctor."

Justin turned to see who had called for him, when a punch landed squarely on his eye. Justin staggered backward, seeking his balance.

"I've got plans for Charlotte," August hissed, his face angry. "She's the prettiest girl in town, and you'd better not be getting ideas about her, what with her working for you. You'd better keep your distance, or else."

It took all of Justin's willpower not to strike August in return. He lowered his hand from his face, stood tall, and his voice was cold as he answered, "Or else what?"

August stepped closer, but Justin didn't flinch. He'd been hit with a cheap shot. He'd like to see August try and fight fairly. Justin knew he'd be able to land just as many if not more blows.

"Or else there's going to be a fire, she and her mother will lose everything, and that will send her right into my arms all the faster. And then," August said, his voice low and menacing, "it will make it all the sweeter once I get what I want. Your pain and suffering, when you realize that you did that to her."

Without another word, August left, and Justin stood there, his heart sinking. Now, any chance he had of telling Charlotte that he was in love with her was gone. He couldn't, not at the risk of her or her mother's safety.

The idea of letting the sheriff know flickered through his mind, but just as quickly he dismissed it. August came from a wealthy and respected family. People like that often got away with anything.

No. The only thing he could do to protect Charlotte was to stay away from her. If he loved her, that's what he had to do.

Chapter 13

"Why won't you tell me what happened?" Charlotte's voice trembled as she stared at Justin. His eye was blackened and swollen.

"I already did," he said, not meeting her eyes. "I tripped on my way home." He set a bag from the bakery down. Even in his hurt state he'd brought them breakfast. She couldn't imagine why.

Charlotte took a deep breath. She doubted what he'd told her. But she also knew he wasn't going to say anything more. When he set his mind to something, he was firm on it. The best thing to do would be to change the subject.

"Mama and I appreciate all the help you are giving to us, both the job and looking into Papa being taken advantage of."

"I'd like to right a wrong, if I can. It's not right that you two have suffered for years. From a previous conversation with your mother, it sounded as though no one had even looked into it or tried." Justin shook his head. "I don't understand that."

"I do," Charlotte said. "People just don't do that. They never have before. We might live in a friendly town, but folks don't get into other folks' business."

He met her eyes, steel in them. Charlotte tried not to flinch at both the anger and the injury. "Have you ever noticed I'm not like others? I don't do things based on what I get in return."

Charlotte took a half step back. "I'm sorry. I didn't..." She stopped. Charlotte didn't know what she'd said that had upset him, but it was obvious he was upset.

"No, I apologize. I'm not myself today," Justin sighed. "Forgive me. I didn't mean to snap at you. My head aches and I didn't sleep well, but that's no excuse."

"There's nothing to forgive," she assured him. "But can I do anything to help your eye? It looks like it hurts."

"It does," he sighed. "But it could be worse. I can see from it, just it's tender and looks terrible. It will be better in a few days, but thank you."

He settled at his desk, and she went to hers as well. The woman who washed their laundry had returned the doctor's bandages and linens that morning, and Charlotte was folding them in the specific way that he liked before placing them into a basket.

While she worked, she let her gaze settle on him. It was clear, despite what he said, that he was out of sorts. He hadn't turned a single page in his medical journal, and he'd been looking at it for nearly ten minutes. Though it was a foolish notion, Charlotte couldn't help but wonder if somehow she had something to do with the way he was feeling.

She hoped not. He'd been so good to her and her mother. She didn't want to hurt him. Not on purpose, and not accidently.

Her gaze wandered around the room, and then through the window. The festival was so close, she could almost imagine herself there. After August had given her the box of candies, she'd decided that he was simply worried about her and the doctor forming an attachment, and that's why he'd been acting childish when they'd spoken for so long in the street. His comments about her staying home and not working weren't a threat, they were a promise, as the wife of a wealthy man.

Still, though she was sure that would happen, Charlotte couldn't help but feel a little bit of sadness at the idea of not getting to see the doctor almost every day. She rather looked forward to their conversations and working side by side with him. In the short time she'd been there, she found she enjoyed her work very much.

But would he miss her when she left? She wondered about that, and thought so, but it was so hard to tell what he was thinking sometimes, especially the last few days. It was obvious something was on his mind.

"Are you...are you ready for the festival?" Justin asked her.

Charlotte glanced up, and couldn't stop the smile on her face. "I am," she said. "I confess, I'm excited. It's going to be the first time I've gone in years."

"I imagine your dress will be stunning," he said. "Didn't you say the fabric was blue? That would suit you well."

"Yes, and Mama helped me to make it. She's a talented seamstress." Charlotte's heart felt light. That morning, she'd decided that the concerns she'd had over August were unwarranted. After all, he'd given her little gifts. That meant he wanted to court. She was simply nervous from her excitement.

Charlotte checked the schedule. No one was scheduled for another half hour. She glanced back at the doctor, who was staring off in the distance. "Are you planning to come?" she asked.

"No," he answered quietly.

Charlotte felt her heart sink. She wasn't sure why. Was it simply because she wanted him to enjoy the day? To be part of the town? Share in its happiness?

"I wish that you would," she told him.

His eyes met hers and seemed to nearly pierce her through. Her heart beat faster, and her stomach felt as though it were spinning.

His voice still quiet, he asked, "Would it make you happy if I did?"

"Yes." Charlotte swallowed hard. Her mouth suddenly felt dry, and she reached for her tea to hide her discomfort. When she set it back down, he was still staring at her.

"Very well, then. I'll go." Justin turned back to his book.

For some reason, his words flustered her. She didn't know why.

The day passed quietly. The patients who came in were all simple cases. A chest cough, a sore head, a laceration. Justin left at lunchtime to check on the Hunters' boy.

Charlotte ate her lunch and then, feeling restless, paced the office. Everything had been done. The office was tidy and neat, the store room shelves organized, the bandages folded, the notes copied. There was simply nothing to do.

A few young girls passed down the street together, stopping in front of the festival poster. Charlotte couldn't help but smile. Years before, that had been her. And now, she was going to be there and choosing the man she wanted to go for a sleigh ride with. It was hard to believe.

Charlotte opened the office door for a little fresh air. Walking past were two women about her age that she didn't know well. Sisters, they'd moved to Spring Falls only a year or two prior. They were talking, and she couldn't help but overhear.

"He says once we ride together in the sleigh, that means we'll be courting. Isn't that delightful?" one asked.

"Oh yes. I'm hoping to catch someone too," the other giggled. "But that man you were talking to, doesn't he have the oddest name? Named after a month! So funny. I've never heard that name before we moved here."

They moved past, and Charlotte smiled. They seemed so happy. But she wondered who would be named after a month! She went through them in her head. March, October, August...

August.

No, not her August.

A wave of nausea washed over her.

Surely the other girl meant someone else. After all, August had given her gifts. Had been jealous about her working for the doctor. Was wanting her to ride with him.

Charlotte sat heavily in her chair. Her head felt light. What was happening?

The doctor entered just then. He turned from hanging his hat on a peg, and then rushed over.

"Charlotte, what happened?" His cool fingers found her wrist as he checked her pulse. "Your heart is pounding. Are you unwell?"

"No, no, I'm fine," she whispered. "I just..." Her voice caught. "I just overheard something I wish I hadn't. I'm sure it wasn't true, but..." She shook her head and shivered. "I'm fine. Everything's fine."

Justin left and returned a moment later with a thick blanket. As he wrapped it around her, she realized it was his blanket. The smell of his soap was strong on it, and he pulled it close to her, kneeling next to her.

Was this what it felt like to be held by him? Her senses filled with his nearness? Him close and protective? It was all Charlotte could do to keep her composure.

"Do you want to rest? You can go upstairs a while," he offered. "Have some tea."

His eyes were filled with such concern, Charlotte could hardly breathe. It struck her then. Never. Never had August felt concerned about her. Not in any of the years that she and her mother had struggled.

The doctor had hardly been here a month, and he'd shown her more compassion and care and tried to help her and her mother—without making it seem like charity. Why?

Oh, yes, she believed him, that he wasn't like others. That he did things because they should be done, but as Charlotte found herself lost in his eyes, the touch of his hands overtop hers as she held the blanket to her, she wondered if there was something more.

And if there was...how difficult of a choice it would be for her. Especially as she'd already told him her heart belonged to August.

Chapter 14

Justin closed his eyes. He felt sick to his stomach. It was a manifestation of his stress, he was sure. How could he have told Charlotte that he'd go to the festival? What was he thinking? He was going to go, and what—stand there and watch the love of his life with another at the festival? Smile and make conversation with the townsfolk, acting as though all were well?

Not likely. But, he'd told her he'd be there, and he'd never break a promise to her. Never.

He was so upset, he'd actually sent Charlotte to run a few errands for him, wanting a few moments to himself. He'd tasked her with a list for the general store, a letter to post in the mail, a lunch order from the diner, and even a trip to the livery, to let them know he'd want his horse later.

None of those things were important. Each of them had been made up. He just needed a chance to pull himself back together. His thoughts had gotten the best of him, and it was difficult to clear his mind. He was a fool. A glutton for punishment, one might say. What was he thinking?

The soft tinkle of the chime over the door rang. It was all Justin could do not to groan. Who was here? He knew he should have locked the door. But, he was the doctor, and so he stood from the chair he'd been slumped upon in the corner of the exam room and forced a pleasant expression on his face.

To his surprise, it was neither a patient nor Charlotte. Instead, her mother stood, twisting her hands.

"Mrs. Harrison," he said, worry filling him over her state. "Are you well?"

She turned to him, and her words tumbled out in a rush. "Doctor, forgive me. I don't mean to push my way into your business, but I can't stand by any longer and watch."

He nodded. "Shall we go to the examination room for some privacy?" He could only assume she meant the matter of August, and what she'd overheard.

"That would be fine," Mrs. Harrison agreed. She took one of the chairs in the small room. Once he'd closed it behind them, she lowered her voice. "Doctor, I know. I know that you are in love with Charlotte. I also know that the gifts she's gotten have been from you, not August."

This wasn't at all what he'd expected her to say. Justin stiffened, though he tried to remain calm. "I beg your pardon?"

I beg your pardon? That was the best he could do? The only thing he could think of to say?

"Yes," she told him. "A mother sees things. You need to tell Charlotte how you feel."

It struck him then. She was twisting her hands and looking anxious because she was upset. Of course she was. Her daughter, one who was both beautiful and of marrying age was working for him. They were alone, and it was likely she suspected him of acting inappropriately.

He had to set things right.

"Mrs. Harrison, I promise you that in no way have I compromised your daughter's reputation," he started.

"And why not?" she asked, surprising him.

"Wh-why not?"

"If you had, then we could have married the two of you, been rid of that horrid August Middleton and whatever plan he has for my Charlotte. You care for her, don't you?"

"I do," he said, panic rising in him. This wasn't a conversation he'd thought to have.

"Then why," she urged, "won't you tell her? Why do you let her think that scoundrel has sent her those thoughtful gifts? You must say something to her. Especially before it's too late."

Justin was silent for a moment. When he looked into Mrs. Harrison's face, all he saw was compassion. It made him want to tell her. To confess everything in his heart.

"My dear boy," she said quietly. "You care so much for her. So, why?"

"I'm not who she wants. It's him, not me," he suddenly burst out, pacing. All of his hurt, all of his insecurities and fears and upset rushed out of him. Now that the flood had started, he couldn't hold it back.

"I'm not rich, I'm not handsome. I have nothing to offer. A doctor with his first practice—a new one at that—in a small town is not wealthy. Why, half of my patients don't pay me in coin, but in service or food. I couldn't give her all she deserves."

"What does she deserve?" Charlotte's mother asked, placing her hands in her lap, while her eyes never left his.

"She deserves someone who loves her. Who can give her what she desires. Who can care for her and protect her and...and I am none of those things." He gestured wildly, hoping his hands would convey his desperation. "The only way that I can protect her is by staying away."

Justin lowered his head and whispered, "If I don't, he will hurt you both."

Bowing her own head, Mrs. Harrison said, "You are far more than you give yourself credit for. You are what

Charlotte needs, and who she would love if she knew you felt the same."

In a quivering voice, she stood and moved to him. "Don't let that August Middleton stop you from what you need to do. He's a bully. I wish I'd said something to my husband before he was taken advantage of. I won't make that same mistake twice, which is why I am here. Never you mind what threats he makes toward me. The sheriff here will protect us if needed."

Justin didn't know how to answer. What was she saying? His head was pounding, and his stomach wouldn't stop churning. For a brief moment, he wished that he'd never even come to Spring Falls. Had he known that all of this was waiting for him, he'd have turned the other way.

But he wouldn't have. Couldn't have. Charlotte was worth even the most terrible of heartache. Her smiles, to him, were such that he'd lay down his life for her.

Or hide like a coward. Was that what he was doing? Letting that bully have his way, in an attempt to protect her?

Justin felt a sudden surge of anger as determination filled him. This woman before him, who had been through so much for so many years, was braver than he was.

No more.

She reached over and squeezed his hands, surprising him. Though she'd been there the whole time, he was so lost in his thoughts he'd forgotten. "You just think about what I've said. That's all."

He stood there watching as Mrs. Harrison left. Justin knew he didn't need to think on what she said. He'd already done that, and decided that Charlotte deserved to know the truth.

He loved her.

Chapter 15

Charlotte knelt over in the store room looking at the small row of bottles before her, whispering their names as she wrote down each. Camphor, willow bark, comfrey, quinine. She carefully checked the levels of each herb, ointment, and medicine on the shelf.

The doctor planned to close the office for half a day on Monday to pick up his supplies in Cottonwood. As today was Friday, and the festival tomorrow, Charlotte hurried to finish helping him make the list before the day's end.

She returned from lunch early to surprise him by getting it finished quickly. He'd not been there when she'd come in, and she assumed he was either somewhere to lunch himself, or perhaps upstairs.

In her neat handwriting, she wrote down the levels of each item on a scrap of paper and made sure to record each item that she felt concern over being too low.

The front office door opened, and Charlotte was surprised to hear August's voice. She was about to step out to say hello when the coldness in his tone stopped her. She was too far away to hear properly, but recognized his mocking laugh.

Her heart beating quickly, she eased the store room door closed and waited behind it. A sudden, perhaps irrational fear formed at the idea of showing herself. She didn't know why, but she was scared to allow either man to see her.

Knowing she shouldn't, Charlotte still pressed her ear near the door, listening.

"How's that eye doing?" August asked, laughing.

Charlotte startled. The doctor had been very careful not to show himself to many people, so how had August known about his eye?

"Maybe I should have blacked the other one as well," he added.

Charlotte sucked in a breath. Justin's injury had come from August? Why had he not told her so? And what had made August do such a thing?

"Did you stop in today simply to ask about my wellbeing?" Justin asked. His voice was just as cold, but his tone was one of refusal to back down.

"No. I couldn't care any less about that. I came to make sure you were keeping your end of the bargain," August said.

"Oh, you mean Charlotte and her mother's safety in exchange for staying away from her." Justin's voice was flat.

What? Their safety? Charlotte didn't understand what he was saying. What did he mean? One hand pressed to the door as she balanced to hear each word.

"So, tomorrow, are you planning to spend the day with Charlotte? Start to court?" Justin's voice, though a little muffled through the door, was still audible.

August laughed again. "You know, I've not decided yet. She's beautiful, but she doesn't bring much to a marriage. She's poor, has an ailing mother, and had a father who let himself be swindled. She can't have much in the way of brains, even if she works in a place like this. There are a few others I've got my eye on. It's easy to have your choice of women if you do it right."

"Why are you telling me this?" Justin's voice was tense. Charlotte felt that way herself. She also felt hurt and angry. There was a roaring sound in her ears, and her hands started to shake.

"Because I can tell it upsets you, Yankee."

August's voice sounded clearer. Had he stepped nearer to the store room? Charlotte hoped neither of them opened the door she hid behind.

"It does," Justin agreed. "I don't like to see my friends treated poorly. Especially when they are good people. By the way, I'm not a Yankee. I'm from Virginia."

"Is that all she is? Your friend?" August sounded curious now, though he ignored the other comment.

"That is none of your business," the doctor said. "I have too much respect for Charlotte to let her know if I had any interest in her when she has her eye on you. I'd never put her in such an unwelcome position."

"I tell you what, if I don't take her, you can have her. Or what's left, anyway. I'll have my fun first." August laughed again. "You're a doctor. You are used to cleaning up messy accidents."

Justin's voice drew closer. He was also right outside the door. What would she do if they came inside? "You don't deserve her. You're an idiot. Charlotte is willing to do anything for you, for your attention and love, and this... this is how you treat her? Talk about her? She needs someone who cares for her. Someone who will defend each hair on her head, who lives to see her smile. Someone who loves her, without fault."

There was a long silence. Charlotte was holding her breath. What was Justin saying? Was that some sort of a confession about his feelings for her? Or was he merely generalizing?

"You..." August paused, and Charlotte could almost imagine him shaking his head, "you are crazy. What's the fun in that? In settling down? Maybe you should be more like me. Then you wouldn't be so upset right now. Look at you! Letting a woman get you riled up?" He laughed, and his voice faded as he seemingly walked away. "Just a game, Yankee."

"Not to me. Maybe it's you who should stay away from her, before I black *your* eyes," Justin growled.

The door leading outside slammed closed, and Charlotte slowly sank onto the floor. Her head swam at the things August had said. He was just leading her along. He had no intentions of settling down. She'd given him her heart, had imagined a future for herself.

She was a fool.

Charlotte closed her eyes for a moment. She'd been so stupid. Had others known this? Overheard his boasts? She was certain they had in a town this small. She would be a laughingstock. Likely already was. Now, she'd have to face everyone tomorrow. Her choices were few. Be humiliated now, or experience it later, when August let everyone know he had no interest in her at all and never had.

And the doctor...Justin. The way he'd spoken about her made her feel a longing, such an intense wish that it was her he was talking about. But it couldn't be. He'd also said she was a friend.

That was all. A friend.

Her heart felt as though it were shattering. No one loved her. No one ever would.

Chapter 16

Justin ran his fingers through his hair. He was filled with frustration, and anger, and irritation, and...well, he wasn't sure what, but he had a lot of emotions going through him right now. Was regret in there somewhere? He was sure it was. Perhaps for controlling his temper.

He hadn't been lying when he'd told August that he had too much respect for Charlotte to put her in any sort of uncomfortable position, be it telling her he cared for her or doing anything else that would make her feel awkward. He had also been telling the truth that Charlotte was a friend. However, she was a friend who he wished was more. Deeply wished was much more.

Justin sighed. Best get to work. Take his mind off of the conversation and the fact that tomorrow was that blasted festival. He glanced about on his desk, but didn't see the list of items he needed to pick up Monday. Charlotte had been working on it, but had stopped before she left to take her lunch break and a walk to the store for something her mother had needed.

The list might be in the store room, so he'd just continue to work on it, if that was the case. He wanted to be sure it was completed by the end of the day.

He reached for the knob and pulled open the door. As he glanced about for the list, a small figure on the floor huddled tightly into herself caught his eye.

"Charlotte?" he said, bending toward her.

Her face, red and swollen with tears, looked up at him. He'd been about to reach for her, to ask if she was okay, but one look and he knew she wasn't. He also knew that she'd likely overheard his conversation with August. How much, he didn't know, but definitely enough to upset her.

"Are you...Can I..." He couldn't figure out what to say.

Charlotte struggled to her feet, and he offered a hand to her elbow to support her. She was trembling and pulled away, and he'd never felt so terrible in his life. Somehow, this was all his fault. His and August's. The one person who he hadn't wanted to hurt, he had.

"Charlotte," he whispered. "Did you..." But he couldn't finish his question.

Her stricken eyes stared at him. "I...I have to go."

"Of course," he said. "Can I—Would you like me to take you home in the wagon?"

She shook her head. "No. No, thank you."

Charlotte pushed past him, and nearly flew out of the office door, barely pausing to grab her shawl and handbag. Justin stood, wondering if he should go after her. If he did, though, what would he say? He threw open the door and raced outside. He looked around for her, but Charlotte was gone. How had she run away so quickly?

His eyes fell on the sheriff's office. That's what he needed. Just who he needed. He could stop by, ask if they'd learned anything about the Harrisons, and then have the perfect excuse to visit Charlotte. To assure himself she was safely home and well.

Physically, anyway. There was no doubt in his mind that her mental or emotional state would be one of difficulty. He felt that way himself.

Justin hurried over to the sheriff's office and walked in. Snow flurries were falling, and he was glad to be inside a warm building.

Sheriff Steele was with the newspaper at his desk and looked up. "Doctor," he greeted.

"Sheriff," Justin answered. "I just wondered if you'd had any more thoughts on the Harrison family."

"Afraid not," the sheriff admitted. "I did some asking around. I know a judge in another town and sent him a telegram. Also checked in with a few other lawmen I know.

Unfortunately, there's not a lot that can be done, since Mr. Harrison willingly signed everything over to his partner."

"I see. I was worried about that," Justin said.

"Sit," the sheriff said, pointing to the chair before his desk. Once Justin had, the sheriff continued, "I do have a friend who suggested we send word around and look for a witness. Anyone who might have overheard the partner boasting or threatening or anything else, just for the chance to get the story in front of a judge. It might work, it might not, it's been so long. However, it might restore even a little bit of what's theirs to the Harrisons."

"That would be something," Justin said. "And very good news."

"It's not a promise," the sheriff warned.

"I understand. But at least it's a spot of hope, in what's been an otherwise dark day."

The sheriff gave him a long look, then asked, "You going to the festival?"

"Ah, no. I mean yes. Maybe. I wasn't intending to go, but I promised someone I would. Not that I'm sure she wants me there now," Justin said, fully aware he wasn't making much sense. He sighed. "It's complicated."

"Some things are," the sheriff agreed.

The office door opened, and the woman Justin had seen before entered. He tried to remember her name. Isabelle, was it?

"Doctor," she said with a smile, then she turned to her husband. "Asher, I've brought you something to eat. Mrs. Donovan insisted you get some of these before they got cold." She set down a small basket then turned to leave.

The sheriff watched her go, then he leaned back in his chair. "You know, I never thought I'd find love. Had run from it for a very long time. Thought I wasn't worthy of it or her. But Isabelle taught me that was far from the truth."

Justin didn't answer. He wasn't sure what to say. Why was the sheriff telling him this?

"Sometimes," the other man continued, "the hardest thing of all is to be brave enough to tell someone when you love them. There's only one thing scarier in life than that feeling of wondering if you'll be rejected."

"What's that? An outlaw coming after you?" Justin asked. He could imagine the sheriff had faced some dangerous times.

"Nope." The sheriff shook his head. "When you realize you're about to lose that person."

Justin stilled. It was true. Wasn't that why he was here? He was looking for an excuse to see Charlotte. Wanting to make sure that she would still talk to him. The difference between him and the sheriff though, well, one of the differences, was that he hadn't lost Charlotte. Not really. He'd never had her. Not in the way he'd wanted.

But they had shared a friendship. That was something he hadn't wanted to lose.

"Sheriff," Justin started.

"Asher," the other man said. "Call me Asher."

He nodded. "Justin, then. I'm wondering, I'm guessing you had that happen. Thought you'd lost the woman you loved?"

"I did," Asher agreed.

"What did you do?" Justin asked.

"I went out and got her," Asher told him.

Was that what Justin needed to do? He planned to stop by her home tonight. But would that be enough to convince Charlotte of both his feelings and of his fear of losing her as a friend or more?

A short time later, as he rode to the Harrison home, Justin wondered when his feelings for Charlotte had become so ineffable.

Chapter 17

"Charlotte? Come downstairs and eat something," her mother urged.

"I'm not hungry," Charlotte answered through the door.

The moment she'd gotten home, she'd flown up the stairs, raced down the hall, and shut herself in her room. She had to. It was the only place she could hide.

There was a small bit of guilt for shutting her mother out. She'd begged several times for Charlotte to tell her what was wrong, but she refused. She couldn't do it. The shame of August's words filled her.

Just a game.

Doesn't bring much to a marriage.

There are a few others I've got my eye on.

How had she been so foolish? She should have seen the signs earlier. The way he'd never really committed to her, hardly talked to her. It had all been her. She'd let herself get swept away in him, or rather in thoughts of him, and had gotten so carried away she hadn't seen the truth.

Then, when she'd seen that terrible side of him on the day he told her he didn't care for the doctor, even though she felt worried, felt doubt, she'd gone and convinced herself it was just another sign of his desire for her, manifesting as jealousy.

None of it was true. What was, was that she was simply a pawn in his little game of heartbreak.

What was worse was that the doctor seemed to know. Justin had been threatened—hurt! And he'd faced both willingly, to protect her and her mother. What threat had August made? And did that mean if she didn't go to him tomorrow at the festival, that he'd follow through on his threat, whatever it was? Or attack Justin again?

She didn't know, and the worry consumed her. Charlotte wanted to protect him, but she also needed to take care of her mother. What was she to do?

There was a knock at her door. She didn't answer. When it sounded again, she answered, "I'm not hungry, Mama. Please. Let me rest. My head hurts."

It was quiet, and Charlotte relaxed slightly. Then, a voice spoke softly against her door. "Charlotte. Please, can we talk?"

She tensed. That wasn't her mother. It was Justin. Why was he here? Charlotte closed her eyes. The ache in her chest grew.

"I don't know what you heard," Justin continued, his voice sounding as pain-filled as she felt, "but I wanted to tell you that I'm sorry. I've never wanted to hurt you, only protect you. From the moment I first saw you, it's been hard to stop thinking about you."

Charlotte looked at the door. Why wouldn't he go away? What made him think he could stay there, torturing her? Making her feel worse? His words were not helping her confusion.

Still, Justin kept talking. "I fell in love with you. I'm not sure when it happened, but I did. I didn't want to tell you, though. You were, are, I don't know, in love with August. It wouldn't have been right of me to make things awkward. It wasn't just that. I enjoy being around you. I was selfish. I was scared to lose your friendship. I still am."

Charlotte bit her lip. She didn't say anything, but she sank down on her bed and pulled her knees to her chest. She rested her head on her knees as she listened.

"And then," Justin went on, "there was the fact you are a single woman. I'm new to town and also unmarried. If I'd let you know how I felt—how I feel—then it could have put you in a compromising position. That would have ruined your chances of getting what you wanted. Who you wanted. Him."

There was a long silence. Charlotte kept staring at the door, trying to picture him beyond it. But no matter how much she wanted to see him, she refused to open that door. Things were too complicated. She hurt too much.

Justin kept talking. "I know that my being scared to say anything, even if I thought it had a noble purpose, has put you in the exact spot I didn't want you to be in. I'm sorry. If I could change things, I would. I just don't know how. Charlotte, you make me happy. Your smile, even if it's not meant for me, does something to me. It brings me joy to see it. Knowing you are content and well and enjoying life, that's all I want. Please, please, Charlotte. I'm worried about you. I just want to make sure you are okay. Please let me see you."

Though he couldn't see her, Charlotte shook her head. She didn't want to see him. Didn't want to see anyone. Somehow, between tonight and tomorrow morning, she had to make up her mind about what to do.

The silence stretched, and Charlotte closed her eyes. Soon the sound of his footsteps faded away.

This wasn't just about her anymore, and what she wanted. This was about her mother and Justin, keeping them safe.

Chapter 18

Through his upstairs window, Justin could hear the excitement rippling through the town as they gathered for the festival. People were set up selling food and drinks, and a large selection of handmade items were for sale as well.

A selection of chairs and chests caught his eye, and he decided to speak with the man and see if a new bookcase could be specially crafted, as his was overcrowded.

Justin shrugged on his coat and buttoned it against the chill in the air. Though it had snowed overnight, the sun was bright and cheerful, and he let himself get swept up in the joyous mood of the town. He stepped carefully, mindful of slippery patches. It wouldn't do for the doctor to need doctoring.

After getting a mug of steaming apple cider, Justin wandered over and talked for a time with the craftsman, then placed an order for his bookcase. When he left there, he spent a short time walking among the people selling delicious-looking treats of all kinds, and settled upon a warm cherry tart.

Leaning against the side of his office, he watched as children ran through the streets with happy shrieks, throwing snowballs at each other. Adults stood in clusters talking and laughing, and young men and women, more than he thought the town had, walked with either nervous or giggly expressions on their faces.

It made him smile to see so many people enjoying themselves. The festival had even brought folks from the outskirts of town. It seemed that everyone looked forward to this event, and had pulled themselves away from their warm homes to come out and enjoy themselves.

As Justin let his eyes take in the sight, he tried to tell himself he wasn't looking for Charlotte. Not specifically. But he was. Deep in his heart he knew that his eyes were seeking her.

He didn't know why he was even there, other than the fact that he'd promised Charlotte he would be. Justin pushed away from the side of his building, fully intending to walk back inside when he saw her.

His breath caught. Charlotte was more than beautiful. She was stunning in a dress made of a deep blue fabric that made her strawberry-blonde curls stand out. She was too far away for him to properly see her expression, but he was glad to know she was there.

Would it be enough to simply watch her? Justin didn't think so. He couldn't. He'd spend the rest of his days loving her, wishing she was his. But he'd blown it. First wasted and then ruined his chance at that. At her.

Not only that, she had refused to open her door when he had finally poured out his heart. All Justin could think about was that she was likely disgusted by him. They'd been friends, she thought, and there he was admitting that he'd fallen in love with her and wanted more.

No, he didn't blame her for ignoring him. She likely thought him abhorrent. Could he blame her? Her employer, pining after her, when she had made it clear her focus and her affection belonged to another.

He had a lot to think about, and a lot to decide about the future. There was a good deal of uncertainty, however, Justin knew one thing—he'd be without Charlotte. She'd made that clear, and his actions had caused the very heartbreak he'd been desperately trying to avoid.

Chapter 19

The entire walk into town with her mother, Charlotte felt numb. It wasn't just the new snow. No, her feeling was one of her emotions, not the weather. Her mother kept glancing at her and finally squeezed her hand. "My dear, you look so apprehensive. Today is supposed to be a day of merriment. Don't let anything bother you. Are you worried about August?"

Then, her gaze turned sharp. "Remember, though he might be interested in you, you don't have to be interested in him. Why, you are a beautiful young woman, and there are many men to choose from, when the time comes that you feel ready for that."

"I know, Mama," Charlotte said. "Perhaps I'm just nervous. It's my first time being here since I was a child."

"I understand," her mother said. "I feel the same. Part of me deeply regrets that we isolated ourselves so much because of the shameful situation we found ourselves in. Perhaps the very people who could have lifted our spirits or helped at the time are the very ones we closed ourselves off from."

Charlotte didn't answer, but squeezed her mother's hand. She could see the lines of worry around her eyes, and hoped that she could ease them. Be that by a courtship with August or not, she wasn't sure, but she did hope to make her mother's life easier.

Right now, everything felt so uncertain. Was there a word that could encompass a situation that was even larger than complicated? She was sure there was, just she didn't know it. That summed up her life at the moment. She didn't know what to do about anything or how to say it.

"My goodness!" her mother said as a wagon loaded with people passed them. Snow was packed down by the wagon wheels, making a little trail. "Look how many people are here."

"I think everyone who has ever lived here is joining in the festivities," Charlotte said, shaking her head in surprise.

It wasn't an exaggeration. The entire main street seemed near to bursting with people. Packs of children ran around laughing and chasing each other with mittens full of snow. Adults stood in clusters looking at the items for sale or enjoying the food. An enterprising individual was selling snow ice cream.

Overnight, it had snowed several inches, which meant the sleighs would soon be gliding through the winterscape, causing red cheeks, joyous laughter, and romance to fill the town. Everywhere the sun hit, the snow sparkled. It looked to be the perfect day.

If only it felt that way.

"I'm going to go set my lace out," her mother said briskly. "We'll find each other later."

Charlotte watched as her mother strode into the crowd and started to unpack the large basket she'd been carrying. It wasn't but a few moments later that women crowded around her mother, holding up pieces of lace. It made Charlotte happy to see her mother looking so proud of her handiwork.

She let her gaze slowly roam over the festival happenings. Was there someone that she knew to say hello to? Her eyes drifted toward the doctor's office. Had...had Justin come? He'd said he would. It would be hard to resist such a gathering.

Except for the fact that he likely thought she was upset at him. In truth, she didn't know how she felt. Seeing the others around her age standing around with either nervous expressions or whispering and giggling made her even more unsure.

All night long she'd worried about what to do. It had all boiled down to her wanting to protect her mother and Justin. If that meant approaching August, even at the risk of her humiliation, then that was what she would do.

August had no idea she'd overheard him boasting and putting her down. A small part of her hoped that was just manly bragging, but a larger part knew it likely wasn't. Each time she thought about the doctor's eye, she shuddered.

Justin. She looked up just then and spotted him. Even through the heavy crowd, their eyes met, and she found herself walking toward him, as though she were being pulled in his direction.

Charlotte stopped in front of him. There was a polite distance, a proper distance, between them. She quietly said, "You came."

"I promised you I would." The look he gave her as he searched her face nearly scorched her through. Charlotte was surprised to find her heart pounding, thundering the way she'd always imagined it would when August asked her to marry him.

How funny that now, she didn't want him at all.

"I'm sorry," he said quickly. "I didn't mean to bring you heartache or complicate things." He ran a hand through his thick hair. "That's the last thing I wanted. What I was trying to avoid."

Charlotte rested her hand on his arm and noticed his eyes follow it. "I know," she whispered, unsure of what else to say.

Justin was unable to hide the pain or the sorrow in his eyes. "About yesterday. I just...just..."

"Just?" she asked softly, sliding her hand down his sleeve to touch his hand.

"Charlotte! Are you coming?"

She turned to see August looking at her expectantly. He looked impatient, and his scowl just about filled his face. Her legs felt frozen to the spot, and not from the snow. As she looked at August, it was almost as though it were the first time she was seeing him.

Her eyes looked past his nice clothing and jacket, his handsome face and perfect hair to what was inside of him. There was no kindness. No respect. No love. He didn't care about her. Not truly. Did he even care for anyone but himself?

"Hurry up," he called again impatiently. "They are about to pull around the sleighs. You do want to ride with me, don't you?"

"Enjoy yourself," Justin said, his voice drawing her attention to the sad smile he wore. "I like seeing you happy." He stuffed his hands into his pockets, and leaned against the side of the building, his shoulders slumped.

Charlotte let herself be pulled away by August, but a strange feeling came over her. She'd longed so much for this day, had looked forward to it...but in that moment, she felt anything but happiness.

Chapter 20

The mayor started telling the story of the event that had started the festival, but Justin wasn't listening. His eyes never left Charlotte, and where she stood near August. He couldn't see her face, but he was sure she was smiling. After all, this was what she'd been wanting. Were they holding hands? He couldn't tell. Someone was standing behind them and blocking his view.

People pushed and worked their way through the crowd, and Justin's lip curled as he noticed several young women making their way closer to August. It was about to be the moment that the couples went on their symbolic sleigh ride. August was now surrounded by young women. Had Charlotte noticed? Surely she had!

Justin wanted to stop watching. To walk away. He wouldn't do that today, but Monday, when he visited Cottonwood Falls, he'd ask their doctor if he knew where else he could open a practice. He'd sell this one. Move away. Start fresh. Get as far away as he could from the only woman he'd ever love.

It would be impossible to stay here in Spring Falls. Not with Charlotte loving someone else.

And how could she love August? Perhaps she hadn't heard anything he'd said. A sickening feeling washed over him. That was it. She'd not heard August at all. She'd...she'd only heard him. His confession.

He was a fool.

If only he'd simply kept his mouth shut.

But no. She'd have found out, eventually.

"Couples!" the mayor shouted. "I hope you are ready! The weather is fine, and we've two dozen sleighs at the ready. Grab your beloved, and line up. We'll do a mile and back, until everyone who wanted a turn got one. You married folk too," he added.

This was it. Justin lowered his eyes. He couldn't watch. Sucking in a shaking breath through his tight chest, he turned to go when someone grabbed his arm.

Justin looked down at familiar fingers. He was scared to raise his head. Afraid to have his hopes up. He stilled, frozen to the spot.

"Justin."

Her voice was soft, but almost commanding. He couldn't stop himself from meeting her eyes. His chest constricted again as Charlotte stood before him.

"I have something to tell you," she said.

Justin braced for it. He knew it was coming and the words she said would stay with him forever, but it was only fair. He'd told her his heart, confessed everything within him. It was her turn.

"It was all you, wasn't it?" she asked. "The ribbon, the candies? Those were gifts from you."

He couldn't deny it. He'd been raised not to lie, but in this instance, when he didn't want to make things worse, Justin simply stayed quiet.

Charlotte continued, "Each thing you did for me, whether I knew about it or not, it was done because you cared for me, wasn't it?"

She took his hands, and he instinctively wrapped his around hers. They were close, and her words were soft, pitched only for him to hear.

"You love me, but you stepped back, because you knew I wanted someone else. That is real love. Justin, I've made a mistake and I hope it's not too late." She looked up at him with a desperation he felt in his very soul.

"No," he told her. "I made the mistake."

Charlotte freed one of her hands and put her finger to his lips. "It's my turn," she told him quietly.

Her soft touch filled Justin with agony. Her hands were warm, despite the snow now falling around them. He was scared to hear what she was going to tell him, and terrified she'd leave too soon. Justin wasn't going to stop her though. He'd bear anything to have her attention focused on him.

"I overheard you and August," she confessed. "And afterward it filled me with confusion. All night I was awake in bed wondering what I should do. While I can't pretend to understand everything the two of you were talking about, I did understand enough. That August had made some sort of a threat to you. And," she added, bringing her gentle touch to his eye, "did this."

"I'd do anything to keep you safe," he told her, his eyes darkening. "Anything."

"Including hiding how much you care for me." She didn't ask it as a question, but presented it as a fact. What else could he say, but yes?

"I've been silly," she told him. "I let myself get swept away in the excitement of the festival, the thrill that someone might be in love with me, and I neglected someone very dear to me, someone who is my closest friend."

Friend. There was that word he'd used. She'd used it as well. Justin started to speak, while simultaneously trying to push away his agony.

"I'm not done," she told him. Charlotte tilted her head and gave him a considering look. "I realized last night that I was so upset and so worried because of you. Because I love you, too. Of all the men here, the one I want to go on a sleigh ride with, and to spend my days with, and to love for the rest of my life is you."

Justin could hardly believe she'd said aloud the words he'd longed to hear. He knew his eyes must be wide and worked to unfreeze his tongue. "I-I'd like that," he finally stammered.

When she smiled at him, an amused look on her face, he tried again. He could do better. "Charlotte," he said, bringing his forehead to hers, "will you be mine?"

Her answer was lost to his ears in the crowd's noisy cheers as the first sled pulled away, but her lips pressed against his were all the answer he needed.

Epilogue

One year later

"Are you almost ready for the festival?" Justin asked.

"I am," Charlotte said. She called then, "Mama? Are you ready?"

"I am," her mother answered, coming down the stairs of their house.

Once called the Harrison house, they now called it the Harrison-Davis house. Charlotte had married Justin a few months prior, and they'd moved into her childhood home. Each morning, he and Charlotte either walked or rode into town to work in his practice. Without fail, every morning he also got her something from the bakery.

At last year's festival, word had gotten around that August had made several threats to families. He ended up not going on a sleigh ride with anyone at all, as Charlotte hadn't been the only one to walk away from him, only she'd done it before the sheriff had arrived.

"Leave or get locked up," were Sheriff Steele's words, and August chose the former. The sheriff wasn't fooling around, and everyone knew it. August had slunk away like a dog with his tail between his legs and his face the color of a tomato. Only, Charlotte's mother had to tell her that part, because she'd been in Justin's embrace and had missed August's embarrassment, and the temper tantrum he'd thrown.

The sheriff recently also had good news for them. A witness had been willing to step forward and tell a judge that he'd overheard Mr. Harrison's partner boasting about having swindled him. It was yet to be decided if anything would come of it, but they all appreciated Sheriff Steele's efforts.

Things were looking up, but even if nothing changed with getting back even a part of her father's business, it didn't matter. Charlotte had all she needed. Justin.

Charlotte wrapped her shawl around herself and stepped closer to Justin and her mother.

"Wait here," Justin said, holding up a hand as Charlotte neared the front door. "I have a surprise."

He hurried outside, and Charlotte and her mother waited. "What do you think it is?" her mother asked, curious.

"I have no idea. All I know is I've not been allowed in the barn for weeks, and people I don't know have been in and out of it!" Charlotte said. She thought about peering through the window, but didn't want to ruin the surprise.

A moment later, Justin opened the door. A huge grin was on his face. "It's ready. Come on out."

As she walked out, neither Charlotte nor her mother could stop the gasps that were pulled from them.

There on the front lawn stood a large sleigh. Two horses were proudly hitched to the front.

"Is this...is this our old sleigh?" Charlotte asked as she ran a hand over it.

"It is," Justin said. He couldn't keep the pride out of his voice. Carefully, he helped Charlotte and her mother into the sleigh, and then leaped in and took the reins.

"Oh!" He reached down under the seat. "I have a gift for each of you."

Charlotte laughed, her voice merry as a smile lit her face. "A ribbon and a box of candy."

"These were from me, in case you were wondering," he said.

"You are a dear," her mother said, holding her own ribbon and box of candies.

"No, I'm just a lucky guy," he said as he shook the reins and the horses started toward town.

"I know it's a year late," he told Charlotte. "But I hope this sleigh ride was worth waiting for?"

Charlotte rested her head on his shoulder. "I'd wait forever, if it meant I got to be with you."

Note from Author

Thank you for taking the time to read A Sleigh Ride for Charlotte!

Could I ask for one small favor? Reviews like yours on Amazon mean so much to me and help others to find my books! Even just a single line means a lot!

Also...

Want a FREE book?

Stop by my website to get your no strings attached **FREE book**. It's my gift to you, as a thank you for reading this one.

www.sarahlambbooks.com

Want to keep reading?

If you enjoyed this story, you might also like Sheriff Asher Steele's story.

Asher's Secret

***

The plan? Pretend he's her betrothed and try not to fall in love.

Sheriff Asher Steele doesn't plan to settle down. Not ever. In fact, he avoids the ladies all together. And he doesn't plan to explain why that is. No one's been able to break through the walls of his emotions and that's just the way he likes it.

But when Isabelle Bowman comes to town with a secret of her own, and a heap of trouble following her, he might be the only one who can help her. What he's not counting on is falling in love along the way and considering opening the walls of his heart to protect her.

Running from her half-brother, who desires nothing more than to kill Isabelle Bowman and take her inheritance, she's desperate for a place to hide. Uninterested in marriage, she thinks the sheriff's idea is preposterous. But she's left with no option. With no funds, a sheriff who thinks she's a troublemaker or a liar, and his plan that will never work, she's sure things are not going to end well.

But could they both be wrong about what the future holds?

https://www.amazon.com/Ashers-Secret-Winning-Devotion-Book-ebook/dp/B0CK5GW81M

***

Also, take a trip over to Cottonwood Falls to meet the other doctor, in Caroline.
Caroline

***

Caroline Watson has been living at Mrs. Hardy's School for Girls since she was orphaned. When forced into marriage by the headmistress, she plots a desperate escape the night before to the furthest place her money will take her.

Even as he tells himself he is uninterested in the beautiful brunette who appeared off the stagecoach like an angel, Dr. Edward Mason finds himself attracted to Caroline. Still, he's determined that no one is going to tempt him into a relationship ever again.

Pushed together, Edward offers Caroline a job. Just as she's comfortable and settled in, a strange man comes to town and follows her. Now she's faced with a choice. Ask for help or run again.

https://www.amazon.com/Caroline-Runaway-Brides-West-Book-ebook/dp/B0B2N32YP5

There are other great books in this series as well!

Find all the Sleigh Ridebooks on Amazon!

Want more of Sarah's books? She writes for children and adults! Find them all on Amazon,
https://www.amazon.com/stores/Sarah-Lamb/author/B098H3SGLK

About the author

Sarah is wife to an amazing teacher and mom to two boys who are growing up just a little too fast. She spends her days working and writing in the Blue Ridge Mountains.